Cherry Blossom

SOTIA LAZU

This book is a work of fiction.

While reference might be made to actual historical events or existing locations, the names, characters, places and incidents are either the product of the author's imagination or are used fictitiously, and any resemblance to actual persons, living or dead, business establishments, events, or locales is entirely coincidental.

Other Books in This Series
Cherry Pop (Vampire Cherry Book 0)
Cherry Stem (Vampire Cherry Book 1)
Cherry Pie (Vampire Cherry Book 3)

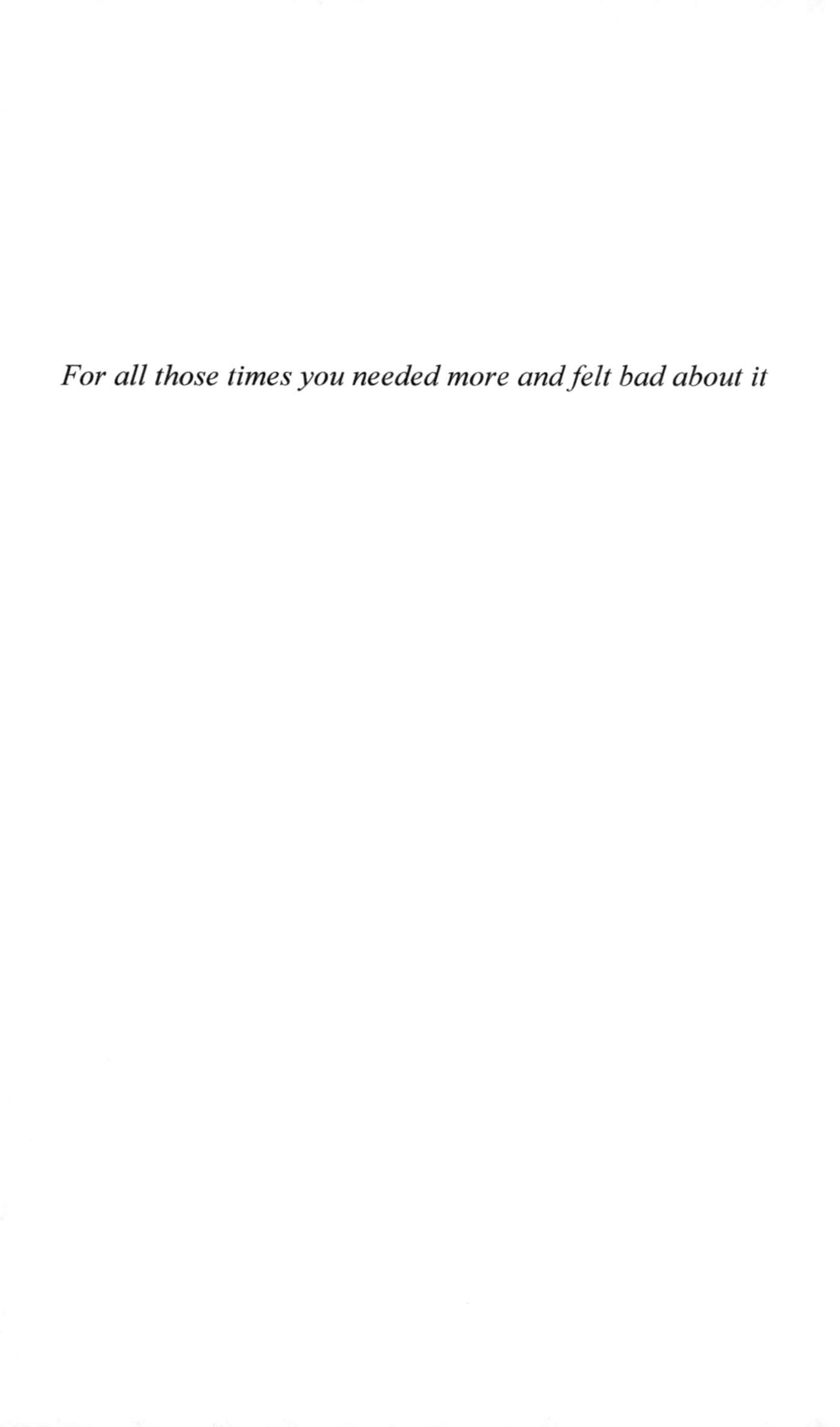

For all those times you needed more and felt bad about it

Table of Contents

Chapter One 1
Chapter Two.. 9
Chapter Three 20
Chapter Four 31
Chapter Five 45
Chapter Six 55
Chapter Seven 62
Chapter Eight 76
Chapter Nine 91
Chapter Ten 100
Chapter Eleven 113
Chapter Twelve 119
Chapter Thirteen 129
Chapter Fourteen 139
Chapter Fifteen 150
Chapter Sixteen 162
Chapter Seventeen 174
Chapter Eighteen 190
Chapter Nineteen 204
Chapter Twenty 221
Chapter Twenty-one 233
Epilogue 247

Chapter One

I like big beds.

I like wide, comfy mattresses that allow me to stretch to my heart's desire and roll over as many times as I please. What's more, I like bedmates that don't take up the space I lovingly maintain around me.

Alex wasn't that kind of a bedmate.

Alex was a cuddler, which I more than appreciated after naughty-times, but suffocated me in my sleep, when the weight of an arm pressed my chest down or a hard body kept me from turning around.

He also snored from time to time, which made no sense, since he no longer needed to breathe. I guess old habits die hard.

I wouldn't have made a big deal out of any of these things this morning, if I didn't wake up to Alex spooning me from behind, both of his arms wrapped around me like steel bars, and his voice whispering in my ear, "I want you to meet my mother."

And I certainly wouldn't have kicked him off the bed, if he didn't add, "And I want to meet your family."

****

"What did you do that for?" Alex rubbed his head where it had impacted with the wall. He was still on the floor where he landed, staring at me.

I sat up and bunched the covers around me, still not fully believing I did what I did—or that he actually said what I heard.

"Cherry? What's up? And *ow*, by the way." He didn't seem as pissed off as I'd be in his place. "Did you have another nightmare? Think I was Willoughby again?"

His concern made me feel bad. To be honest, I never had nightmares of Willoughby. At times when Alex was too clingy in my sleep, however, I may have elbowed him in the ribs or kicked him in the shin and afterward implied I thought he was my maker, haunting my dreams. He was having nightmares of his turning too, so he believed me.

I shook my head. "Not him," I said. "Different nightmare. About you wanting us to meet each other's folks."

That got him fuming in no time, which worked out quite well, because I wasn't feeling all lovey-dovey.

"Why's that so bad? My mother's been hearing about you for two months now. She wants to meet you." And *this* was a glaring example of why we should let our family think we died after our turning. If the vampire council caught a whiff of Alex's staying in touch with his mother, they might resort to extreme measures.

Then again, they'd have to know he was a vampire, for them to even care, so it was a moot point. After the havoc that resulted to his turning, the vampire council reinstated the Vampire Social Services, to help tighten the bonds within our community. They also decreed a census, to record all vampires currently in the United States. We'd kept Alex's change in status a secret, to avoid dealing with the repercussions of breaking the law against turning new fledglings.

"What if she doesn't like me?" 'Cause loveable as I am, this was always a possibility. I didn't voice my worries that I might not like her. "And you can't meet my family. *I* can't meet my family again. They think I'm dead."

"They think you're missing. Finding out you're still"—he scrunched his face—"*around* would be the greatest thing to ever happen to them." He was using his rational voice on me, something that probably worked when he interrogated suspects, but which I hated when I was feeling unreasonable. He got on his feet and dusted plaster off his hair. "And my mom will love you. Just like I do."

Yeah, okay. Play the *I-love-you* card, why don't you? "We'll talk about it," I said. "I'll ask Constantine what he thinks. He knows the council better than I do, and they like him." If they didn't, they'd have publicly executed him for admitting to killing two of their own. Instead, they had him join them. "If he thinks it's safe for me to go home, we'll visit my family."

There was no way my ex would condone something like this. It was reckless and might endanger us all—plus he might be acting cool and superior, but I could tell he wasn't happy with my relationship with Alex.

Alex must have realized Constantine would say *no*, because he kicked dejectedly at the floor and came back to bed with a scowl on his face. "I'll talk to him too. Maybe I can convince him," he said, standing in front of me in his birthday suit.

He could certainly try. Meanwhile, I'd do my best to make him forget about the whole thing.

I smiled, slid to the edge of the bed, and let the covers drop, to reveal a state of undress that matched his. I traced the lines of his body—hard muscle under soft skin that shivered ever so slightly under my touch.

His gaze was locked on mine, as I replaced my fingers with my mouth down his stomach. I loved the texture, the smoothness of his skin. I feathered my lips along his hipbone and felt his legs tremble. I loved his body's involuntary responses. Smiling to myself, I brought one hand around him and dug my nails into his buttock, pushing him against my face.

He rudely interrupted my efforts at driving him crazy with anticipation, by stepping back, grabbing my knees, and laying me flat on the bed in one smooth move. Before I could voice my protest, he was kissing me.

I arched upward and wrapped my legs around his hips, but he resisted, his body hovering above me. "No." The single word was heavy with promise.

He kissed me again, teasing my mouth open with his tongue and finding mine. The kiss deepened, as did my need for him. When he sucked on my lower lip, I ran one hand down the length of my body and between my legs, where I wanted him the most.

He closed his fingers around my wrist and forced my hand to the mattress. "Be a good girl and don't move." His cool breath tickled my ear.

It's not like me to submit without a fight, but the lust burning in his gaze stifled my rebellious side. I tangled both hands in the sheets, to keep from touching him.

His mouth moved down the side of my neck, kissing and licking the area over my jugular. I wanted him to bite me. I wanted to push against him. I held back. He barely let a fang graze my skin and chuckled at the whiny sound that escaped my throat.

The bastard.

He made his way down my body with his lips and fingers, pulling sighs and moans out of me with every kiss, every caress, every nip. My nipples hardened at his touch. My stomach tightened. Every nerve in my body screamed for more, but he refused to give it. By the time his face was at the apex of my thighs, I craved him beyond reason. I couldn't be held accountable for my actions if he didn't sink inside me immediately.

Only Alex wasn't done teasing me.

He closed his teeth over the sensitive flesh at the inside of my thigh without breaking the skin, and sucked while pushing a finger inside me.

My hips flew off the mattress, and my eyes watered at the pressure building up in my belly. I needed just a bit more. More pressure. More friction. I needed him to add another finger and pump them both. I needed him to eat me out. I needed him to—*Oh God...*

He didn't do what I wanted but he didn't withdraw, either. Instead, he splayed the fingers of his free hand on my stomach to hold me down and pierced my skin with his fangs at the same time he pressed his thumb on my clit.

I thought I was going to scream, but only a hoarse whisper reached my ears when I managed to form a word. "Please."

He either didn't hear me or ignored me. He drew lazy circles with his thumb around my clitoris and slid his finger in and out so slowly, I couldn't get the *more* I needed. He kept pulling at my blood, and the sensation was enough to drive me to the precipice but not to throw me over.

Pleading obviously didn't work, so this time I went with an order. "*Now.*"

Alex was not in a compliant mood. He stopped touching me entirely and raised his gaze to mine, making sure I watched as he licked his lips. Once he had my undivided attention, he lowered his head again and slowly ran his tongue along my cleft.

That was when I stopped being nice.

I grabbed his hair to anchor him to me and began grinding against his face, urging him to go faster. Harder. If he wanted to play *Hold off Cherry's Release,* I'd take matters in my own hands.

I was so close—so *fucking* close—when he forcefully removed my hands from his head and rolled me over.

Now we're talking.

The bed was too tall for my knees to reach the ground, and my legs dangled awkwardly. I tried to find purchase on the floor with my toes, but Alex nudged my thighs apart with one knee, throwing me completely off balance, and pushed inside me.

Can't say I complained about the manhandling. Perhaps I would have, if I weren't enjoying it so much. I've always loved seeing Alex's mild manners put aside and this dominant side of his come out in the bedroom—bathroom, kitchen, public place, wherever.

He dug his fingers into my hips and lifted me to meet his thrusts. I didn't have time to push my body up with my arms. My face was rubbing against the mattress, but all I felt was the fire he stoked inside me with every plunge. Every time he withdrew, I clenched around him, trying to lock him and the pleasure in place. My fangs popped out, and I bit at the sheets, uncaring that I'd leave holes in them. I was nearly there nearly there nearly—

Alex's movements turned jerkier, shorter. He draped his body over mine, letting go of my hips so he could wrap his arms around my torso. I let him draw me to him and tilted my head to the side, to get my hair out of the way.

The moment his fangs pierced my throat, everything I wanted, everything my body craved for suddenly flooded my senses, short-circuiting my brain. I couldn't tell which of us was trembling. All I knew was that, pinned to him, torn sheets hanging from my mouth, I felt my body shudder with waves of pleasure until I could no longer keep my eyes open.

Alex obviously had problems controlling himself, too, because his knees buckled, and we toppled forward, his teeth and cock still inside me.

In my fuzziness, I barely registered his tongue gently licking the wounds he'd inflicted, before he rolled to the side and gathered me close. It's possible I purred with delight. This was one of the times I not only didn't mind the cuddling but welcomed it.

I don't know if I drifted off or just zoned out, but I'd been too engrossed in my efforts to distract him, to realize someone else was in the room.

Until Constantine cleared his throat.

Chapter Two

Asking my ex if he'd watched my current lover and me having earth-shattering sex would lead to all kinds of awkwardness, so I opted for yelling at Constantine to get out of the room and go wait for us in the kitchen.

He left with the huff and flourish that accompanied him since he became a member of the vampire council.

"Come on, before he pitches a fit." Alex tossed my jeans and a top on the bed.

I ignored the clothes and watched him slide into his own jeans. The sight made up for the cramped sleeping arrangements. "He can wait." I stretched on my back and reached with my toes for one of his belt loops. "I think you should come back to bed."

"And I think you should stop avoiding him." He was right. I was avoiding Constantine. I bet Alex didn't know why, though.

I wasn't sure why I did it. I only knew I felt odd being couple-y with Alex in front of my ex. It was like I rubbed his face into my happiness with a man who wasn't him. The lingering looks Constantine gave me from time to time didn't help much, either. They weren't looks of longing. He studied me, as if dissecting me. Trying to read my mind. He never said a word against Alex—or *for* him, to be honest—but his general disposition had turned snarkier. Gloomier. Not that he'd been a ray of sunshine to begin with, but sensing I was the reason for his change made me feel bad.

"I can't deal with his smartassness first thing in the morning," I said. Pulling the covers over my head acted like an end to the conversation. Or so I thought.

Alex drew the covers away and leaned over me, now fully dressed. "Get up. Stop being a five-year-old. He may have something important to tell us."

He had a point. Constantine or his people—council members always have *people*—might have finally spotted Willoughby. With a groan meant to show my displeasure, I got up and put on my clothes. "Let's go," I said and led the way.

****

Constantine sat at the table, entirely out of place in the spacious, well-lit kitchen. It wasn't his age that put him at odds with the modern tiles, shiny lacquered-wood and glass surfaces, and metal elements. He looked mid-thirties and hot, his long blond hair framing an angular face devoid of wrinkles. Only his blue eyes betrayed he'd seen much more than his smooth skin and casual attire indicated.

His jeans and white T-shirt weren't too stylish for him to be in a place where food was prepared and served, so that couldn't be it either.

Eyes narrowed, I studied him until realization sunk in. It was his posture that made him clash with the surroundings. He held his back straight, shoulders square, and chin up, as though he were royalty sitting on his throne, waiting for peasants to bring forth their offers.

I *so* wouldn't be one of them.

"Nice of you to finally join us," he said.

"Like we had a choice." I'd *known* he'd be sarcastic. I should have come up with a reply that had more bite.

Liza, who was never too far from Constantine, threw me a scolding look from her perch on the kitchen counter, her black eyebrows furrowed. She was absolutely gorgeous and had been an aspiring model when my old talent agent delivered her to my maker, who wanted to add her to his undead army of models.

Alex, Constantine, and I rescued Liza and two other fledglings from Ádísa and her cohorts. Constantine took the girls in, and they more or less worshipped the ground he stood on.

Now I itched to tell Liza I'd been in Constantine's life much longer than she had, and could therefore speak to the man she viewed as a god any way I pleased, but it seemed petty. Instead, I returned her look and took a seat across from my ex. Alex pulled out a chair between us, turned it around, and straddled it.

"Talk," I said to Constantine.

"Would you like something to drink first?"

I looked around. "Where's Wesley? I could go for some coffee. And maybe eggs." Constantine's human butler and his incredible cooking skills were among the perks of living at the mansion. Normal food doesn't sate our hunger, but we enjoy the hell out of it.

"Wesley is busy. Liza has brewed tea."

"Then no, thanks."

Next to me Alex shook his head. "I'm good. What's up?"

"There has been a possible sighting of Willoughby." Constantine motioned at Liza, and she hurried to refill his teacup.

Gag.

"I can't say more at this time, but you should be getting ready for a trip at short notice," he said.

Alex nodded, unperturbed as always by Constantine's exaggerated air of mystery.

I wasn't that big a person. "You got us out of bed to tell us someone's seen the bad guy, but not who or where? What's next?" I deepened my voice to a basso. "It will rain one day in the near or distant future." In my normal pitch, I asked, "Was that doomsday-worthy enough for you?"

"Cherry, this is all I can tell you right now. You have to trust me. What matters is we may have a clue as to his surroundings, if not his intentions."

"A clue you won't share with the class."

"I'm sure he'll tell us more when he knows more." Alex placed one hand over mine, which I'd apparently fisted without realizing it. His effort at soothing me had the opposite result.

"He knows more now." I locked my gaze on Constantine's. "Don't you?"

Constantine shook his head and smiled ruefully. "When did you become so cynical?"

I scrunched my face in mock concentration, then widened my eyes. "*I know*. Must have been about the same time I found out you lied to me and our relationship was a sham. Yup, that was the exact moment."

His eyes were a stormy midnight blue that usually meant anger or extreme pain. Yes, the man came with preinstalled mood-rings on his face.

I wasn't being fair. His maker had appointed him my sponsor. She wanted me to fall for him, and it hadn't taken long for that to happen. But at the time, Constantine didn't know Ádísa had ordered my turning. And contrary to her wishes, he'd really loved me in return. Weeks ago, he insisted he still did.

Liza walked up behind Constantine and laid both hands on his shoulders. Until that moment, I'd only thought of her as Head Concubine. I'd assumed all they shared was sex and blood. Apparently, I'd been at least partially wrong there.

How well she knew him astounded me. Though Constantine's posture didn't change, Liza noticed the subtle increase of tension in his body, like I did. Thing was, I couldn't tell if Constantine's discomfort was out of guilt over the lies he'd told me in the past—for which he'd atoned by killing his own maker—or because he really knew more about Willoughby than he let on.

I didn't want it to be the latter. Not when he'd been regaining my trust. My stomach clenched at the possibility. Instead of asking him, I said, "Fine, be mysterious. But while we're here, can you remind Alex we're not supposed to keep in touch with our families?" Might as well get one problem out of the way.

The tiny lines of tension around Constantine's eyes smoothed out, and he relaxed his jaw. Was it me, or did my ex seem relieved by my change of subject?

Before Constantine could speak, Alex piped in. "I want Cherry and me to meet each other's folks. I know it's not something vampires do, but I'm still alive as far as my mother knows, and I don't see how Cherry's family would be anything but ecstatic to see her again. She was never declared dead, just missing, so she can tell them she was off finding herself or something."

I didn't expect the matter-of-fact way he'd presented his case to do him any good. What he was asking went against council policy. No way would Constantine condone it.

Constantine smiled, his irises now faded to their normal light blue. "We have been doing things our own way for a while now." He shrugged, apparently oblivious to how my mouth gaped at his response. "I don't see why you shouldn't do as you please, as long as you're careful. I will, however, be joining you when you visit Cherry's parents. As a precautionary measure, in case things go awry. I'll have to make some arrangements first, but we should be able to leave by the end of the week."

It was obvious from Alex's eager expression that he'd go along with anything to get the go-ahead for his silly fantasy. I didn't exactly view things the same way. It was weird how readily Constantine had agreed.

"Precautionary measure?" I asked. "You plan to mind-wipe them, if our little reunion is threatening to the vampire community?" Meaning if my parents somehow realized I was undead, freaked out, and threatened to tell the world about our existence.

The look he gave me was full of scorn. "No." The word sounded like it was mentally accompanied by several non-flattering adjectives. "What I had in mind was that you'll have a member of the council with you, in case another vampire realizes what you're up to. My presence will make your visit legitimate." I could swear I heard him finish his sentence in my head with, "You idiot."

"Oh." Because, what else could I say? He only had our best interest at heart, and I really should stop being so suspicious of him. If he said it was all right, it probably was. "Okay then, I guess."

Constantine grinned. "Besides—the three of us on a road trip? Think how much fun it will be."

Yeah, he was hiding something, all right. All this cheer wasn't normal. "What's in it for you?" I asked.

"Just the pleasure of your company." His mocking tone and arched eyebrow didn't exactly vouch for his sincerity.

"And what else? Why come with? If you plan on hurting my parents—"

He slammed one hand on the table, making all of us jump. Outbursts were no more like him than cheeriness was. "I'm not planning on hurting anyone, you stubborn woman. I'm coming with, because you'll need me there."

I had no response for that.

Liza's face fell. "Can't I come with you?" Her big green eyes shone with unshed tears. She was really going to cry, because Constantine would be away for a few days? Or because he'd be with me?

But I had a boyfriend…who was glaring daggers Constantine's way. Oh-kay.

Constantine tugged at Liza, until she rounded the chair and faced him. "You know Carrie and Sally need you," he said, his tone grave. "*I* need you to stay behind and take care of our girls."

She preened at his show of trust, and I felt bad for her. I'd been there, ready to do anything for his approval. I hoped it ended better for her.

****

For all his outstanding qualities in and out of bed, Alex wasn't above snarking.

"So I ask nicely, but all it takes for you to agree is Constantine's permission. Good to know," he said with fake cheer, as soon as our bedroom door was closed behind us.

"Thought you got what you wanted." I turned my back to him, kicked off my slippers, and went to the closet in search of my sneakers. I'd promised Sheena I'd catch a late movie with her, and I'd rather focus on that than what Alex was saying.

"No. Constantine got me what I wanted. And you said nothing when he said you'd want him there."

"He said I'd *need* him there, and he's right. He knows our laws better than me, and he can protect us from the rest of the council. You were the one who thought talking to him about it was a good idea."

He shoved his hands in the pockets of his jeans and rolled his head from side to side. "Yeah… I'm being an ass. I'll call my mother and tell her we'll go by tomorrow evening. She can't wait to meet the girl I'm constantly talking about."

Oh, *goodie.* With or without Constantine's approval, the idea still held no appeal. "Isn't it too late for you to call her? Maybe you should do it in the morning and give her a couple days' notice."

"Notice for what? She'll just be making dinner."

My right sneaker was in front of me, but I couldn't see the left one. I crouched down and started rummaging through the shoes that littered the floor of my closet. "I don't know. *Notice.* Where is the stupid thing? Sheena will kill me if I'm late."

Sheena wouldn't say anything, even if I stood her up. She still felt guilty for being the one to introduce me to Willoughby, though she didn't know what he was at the time.

Alex walked up behind me, bent down, and closed his hand around the second of my shoes, as if by magic. "My mother's always ready for guests," he said, holding it out to me.

I grabbed it and squeezed my foot inside without bothering to undo and redo the laces. "Call her in the morning." By then, I might have found an excuse to avoid that get-together. With a quick peck to his lips, I rushed to the door. "We'll talk when I'm back. We're meeting the guy from the blood bank after the movie, so I'll bring some blood home. Maybe you can try it?" He still refused to drink human blood, saying vampire blood kept him sated for a longer period of time.

I believed he saw drinking human blood as the last step to no longer being human.

Fast as lightning, Alex pinned me to the door, his body hard against my back, his arms framing my shoulders. "I only want *your* blood," he whispered harshly, his face in my hair. His erection digging in my back was the least of my concerns.

"Okay, the mood swings? Not doing it for me. You go from mellow to seeing red in no time. Is something bothering you? If you want to talk about it, I can call Sheena and cancel." I prayed he said yes and finally talked to me about how he really felt about being a vampire. He'd told me how powerless he'd felt when Willoughby drained him—how he hated the fear and the nightmares that followed—but not a word about what he'd become.

He pumped his hips against me. "It's bothering me that you're not naked."

Trying to fuck issues away was my thing. Alex usually insisted it solved nothing. Seeing him resort to the same cheap trick raised a wave of anger inside me.

Let go," I said. "I have a show to catch."

He stepped back, and when I turned, his arms were up. Whether in surrender or resignation I couldn't say. Something clenched in my gut. His lack of a heartbeat wasn't the only thing different after his turning. I wanted to believe the rest of the changes I saw in him would smoothen out, as he got used to his new reality.

I pulled him down by his shirt and whispered, "Be good."

Then I touched my lips to his once more and went to find my friend and ex-manager.

Chapter Three

The movie was nothing noteworthy, but mind-numbing and jolly was exactly what I needed for my head to clear. By the time the ending titles rolled, I'd decided to let things unfold as they would. I'd meet Alex's mother and bring him to my childhood home. My lifespan would be too long for me to worry about every little thing.

My stomach clenched at the thought of facing my parents, but I put on a huge smile. "You up for ice cream? I'm buying." Actually, Constantine was. Since he'd achieved council member status for something we'd both done, he was giving me half of the stipend that came with the position.

Sheena arched an eyebrow, her dark eyes glinting. "How very generous of you."

Pretending not to notice the sarcasm in her voice, I smacked her ass. "You want lobster, you got to gimme some sugar."

She kept a straight face, but I could see a grin tilting the corner of her lips. "Tempting though it may be, I'll have to refuse. Ice cream will do."

By now, we'd reached the ice cream stand. "One of those." Sheena pointed at the largest cups available. "I'd like two scoops of caramel and one each mocha and vanilla."

"I want a cone, straight up chocolate, please," I said.

The teen behind the counter asked if we wanted any toppings. I refused, but Sheena hid her ice cream under thick layers of whipped cream and added a cherry on top. How the woman remained slim was beyond me.

"You're a cheap date." I indicated her cup with a tilt of my head.

She shook her head, glossy black curls bouncing. "And you're using cheesy lines that send the feminist movement decades back. How you got not one, but two gorgeous vampires to fall for you is beyond me."

"They're old fashioned. I just smiled and nodded a lot."

"I see. Now it all makes sense. *Hey.*" She batted my hand away when I tried to pinch the maraschino that crowned her humongous dessert. "So, you and Alex are meeting the in-laws, huh?"

"Don't wanna talk about it." To stress how *much* I didn't want to, I stuffed my face with more ice cream.

"Wanna talk about how your new and old beau are disconcertingly civil with each other?" So she'd noticed too. If I were still human, those two would give me heartburn.

"Would such a discussion entail hypotheses of a future threesome with said beaus?"

She took her time cleaning drops of vanilla from her hand with her tongue. "I doubt it."

"Then no."

"Okay, you choose the subject."

I gave it a moment of consideration. It had been a long while since Sheena and I last had a girls' night out. Hell, longer since we'd been friends.

She'd shown up at the bakery I worked for when I first moved to L. A. and offered me a job. She helped me lose weight, managed my career, and soon became my only friend.

She'd also been the one to hand me and the three vampettes now living with us to Willoughby and his associates. She'd been afraid for her life, and her remorse was genuine. Since she'd moved into Constantine's mansion, she'd been doing her best to help the fledglings. I'd finally accepted her apologies, and we were rebuilding our friendship from scratch. That night in the city was supposed to help us bond over silliness—and possibly alcohol.

I didn't want to be a party pooper and ruin the fun mood, but I had nobody else to talk to. "I'm worried about Alex," I finally said. "He insists everything is fine, but won't touch human blood."

"Isn't that a dietary choice?"

I shook my head. "It's more than that. It's like he resents having to feed off humans—which is totally rational, only he has to get over it at some point. I'm not saying he should go killer-sucker. I just wish he'd seem more at peace with his new nature. Being with him is like riding a roller coaster."

"Are we talking about the crazy vampire sex?" She stuffed a spoonful of caramel in her mouth, but not before I saw her smirk.

I glared. "I'm serious. Lately he seems ready to snap at the smallest thing, and I believe it's because he can't accept himself."

Her gaze softened. Lost its teasing edge. "And you feel guilty."

"And I feel guilty." I forced that new nature on him. He never had a chance to refuse it. Not having consented to my own turning, I hated that I hadn't given him a choice.

"My poor idiot." Sheena held her ice cream away from her body with one hand and pulled me into an awkward hug with her free arm. "You saved his life." I started to protest, and she shushed me. "So he's brooding a bit. Beats being dead. If he can't deal with his current existence, there are always exit strategies."

I pulled away. "I'm not killing him."

"I'm not saying you should. I'm saying he's a grown man who knows his options. If he doesn't feel like being the evil dead, he can take a nap on a park bench right before sunrise. That he hasn't so far means he's dealing. It'll take a while until he's fully there. Now let's go see Blood Guy and get home. I need to pee."

"You have such a way with words."

"It's a burden, but I carry it with elegance."

"Obviously. But maybe you should sit somewhere and wait for me? Somewhere with a ladies' room, so you don't have a little accident? The meeting place is more than a couple of blocks from here."

She shook her head. "Better idea—you fly me home, I make Margaritas and wait for you?"

"Only if you're sure you won't pee on me."

"Oh, shut up. I'm a lady."

Laughing, we walked into an alleyway, and I did my vamp-lift-off thing. It's really nothing more than willing your body to rise above the ground, but it only works if you believe you can win a fight against gravity, and not all of us are open-minded enough to manage it.

Sheena made a run for the bathroom as soon as we landed at home, and I took off again for my meeting.

****

Blood Guy, known to his friends as Frank, was a blood bank employee and my first success story in compelling. He was the first person I'd ever managed to use my vampire gaze on without turning him into a complete puppet or making him think I was crazy. In his mind, I worked for a hazardous materials disposal unit. I called, and we met behind the bank, where he handed over bags of blood that needed to be destroyed for whatever reason.

I'd only been using him sporadically in the years since Constantine had taught me how to feed from live donors without endangering them. With four fledglings to keep fed and happy, however, I'd recently added Frank's number to speed dial.

"You're late." He checked his watch, as if to make sure he had it right.

"I know. I'm sorry. You know how it is."

He nodded, though he had no clue how it was, or what *it* meant. He always nodded, because we always had the same dialog. I hadn't compelled him to greet me that way every time he saw me; I guess creating a pattern in our transactions reassured the rational part of his brain.

"You park close by?" he asked. "Bag is heavy." That too was part of our usual rapport.

"Round the corner." I took hold of the dark blue duffel he carried. "Thanks."

"Sure you don't need me to help with that?"

"Nope. Got it. Thanks again."

"See you next month."

I gave him a little wave and waited until he was back inside the building. As soon as I was certain I was completely out of his field of vision, I kicked at the ground and was airborne.

I entered the mansion from the basement and stowed the blood in the freezer Constantine had installed in the en-suite I shared with Alex. That floor housed our room, the gym, and the huge-ass bedroom and white-marble bathroom Constantine shared with the three fledglings, while the upper floors of the mansion boasted two living rooms, four and a half bathrooms, a kitchen, and a *parlor*—let alone Wesley's apartment. When I asked Constantine how come he didn't want a more livable basement apartment for the daytime, he said we weren't supposed to live during the day. Bleak, huh?

I pulled my red hair back in a ponytail, secured my annoying fringe to the side with a bobby pin, and rushed upstairs. The whirring of the Margarita maker acted as a homing beacon, leading me to the kitchen.

"I'm home," I said as I entered the room. "Bring on the booze."

"Thought you wouldn't be back till later." Alex leaned against the stove, arms crossed over his chest.

"Oh, hi. Yeah, didn't Sheena tell you? We decided to do the alcohol-binge part of the night here." I approached and rose on my tiptoes to plant a kiss on his lips. He didn't return the greeting. "Is something wrong?" I looked around. "Where's Sheena?"

"Needed to get something. Asked Wesley to drive her. She'll be back soon."

I took a step back. He looked tense, and there was some sort of menacing wave coming off him. His eyes seemed cloudy, like he wasn't really seeing me. I wanted to touch him but refrained. I'd never before felt unsettled in his presence. Now it was as if he'd raised some sort of force field around him.

"Alex? Everything okay? Are you hungry?"

He shook his head and smiled, but the sense of wrongness was still there.

I wasn't afraid of him. He was my Alex. He was dealing with things his way.

I was relieved to hear footsteps behind me. "I heard the car," Constantine said. "Sheena is back, so let's leave the ladies to it, Alex. We can spar, if you feel up to it." He was training Alex to control and utilize his superhuman strength, but the two never let me watch.

"Yup, you should go," I said with false cheer. "I won't be too late. Wanna catch up on some girly stuff." And maybe shake off the weird feeling suffocating me.

Constantine placed his hand on the small of my back, and I let out a sigh. Whatever his reason for doing it, to me it meant he realized I was uncomfortable, and reminded me he was there for me. Little things like this made up for his snark and his occasionally sour disposition.

Alex grabbed the front of my shirt and pulled me to him. Before I could react, he closed his lips over mine and pushed his tongue into my mouth in a kiss that felt more like raw hunger than love. "See you in bed." His eyes were clear now, and the roughness of his voice sent goose bumps of the nice kind down my spine.

Lust and unease fought inside me, making my gut clench. "Yes, Mr. Caveman." Once I regained my balance, I turned and followed the two men out with my gaze, enjoying the view. Even the compounded yumminess of their broad shoulders and narrow hips didn't calm my nerves, though.

Something had really been off there for a while, but as long as Alex was crazy about me, nothing was beyond fixing.

Sheena ducked inside. "Is it safe to enter now?"

"When wasn't it?"

"When male bravado had replaced the oxygen in the room." I arched both eyebrows, and she went on. "Remember how your beaus were insufferably polite to each other?"

"Yeah…"

"Well, you can forget it. Don't know exactly what they were talking about, when you dropped me off, but they seemed a heartbeat away from pulling their cocks out and measuring them—not that it'd be an objectionable sight, but you catch my drift."

"They were fighting?"

"More like posturing and staring each other down. I asked if we had fresh strawberries, and they all but growled at me. I found what I was looking for and started making our drinks, but then Alex pushed Constantine away, and Constantine grabbed him by the throat, and I had to sneak out and beg Wesley to drive me around for a while. Even the vampettes stayed away, and you know how they go gaga over topless Constantine."

"Constantine was topless?"

"Because that's what you need to focus on?" She flicked my ear with one long, lime-green fingernail. "Those boys are playing nice when you're around, but they need to realize they're both parts of your life now. Either that, or one of them has to stop being part of it."

I didn't want to think about the latter, but starting a conversation out of the blue about how they both meant a lot to me—*in different ways*—seemed stupid. "Maybe the field trip will do us all some good?"

"Field trip?"

"Ah huh."

"The three of you?"

"Yuppers."

Sheena cracked a smile. "You really are trying for that threesome, aren't you?"

Though it wouldn't be the worst possible outcome I could fathom, as far as the three of us were concerned, my hopes for the trip were simply that the two men in my life would do some bonding, and I'd get some peace of mind.

Sheena didn't seem very convinced when I said so.

The first Margarita mix had turned into watered down slosh, so we made a fresh one and proceeded to consume it with the fervor of college kids on their spring break.

****

Alex was already in bed, when I turned in for the day. The smell of his shower gel wasn't strong enough to disguise the smell of blood. His blood. I guessed his sparring with Constantine hadn't exactly been tame. Maybe that was good. If they resolved their issues on the training mats, everyday unlife would run more smoothly.

He turned and pulled me to him as soon as I was under the covers, and I let my body melt in his embrace. The alcohol I'd imbibed was sufficient to give my vampire constitution a pleasant buzz and dull my worries. "Are you okay?" I whispered. "Sheena said—"

"Shh. Sleep." He touched his lips to the side of my neck and tightened his grip around my waist.

I hugged him back, resting my head on his unmoving chest. "I can't. I'm worried. I know Constantine isn't your favorite person, and you certainly aren't his, but this is his place, and we need him." Alex tensed, and I ran my fingers along his brow. "For now at least. He's really not that bad, once you get used to him. What happened between the two of you today, anyway?"

"Don't worry about it." He caressed the side of my face. "It'll be fine. Now can we please get some sleep? I'm beat."

He hadn't exactly answered my question, but I felt hopeful. I kissed his collar bone. "'Kay. Goodnight. I love you."

"Love you too."

That was all that should matter.

Chapter Four

I woke up with Alex inside me.

He'd often used his mouth or fingers to tease me awake in the past, but never his cock.

Now I found myself lying on my stomach, Alex sliding in and out of my pussy in slow, deep strokes. I smiled. *The perfect wakeup call.* I tried to turn and look at him over my shoulder, but he twisted one hand in my hair and pushed my face to the pillow.

So we were playing rough. *Nice.*

I tilted my hips upward. The angle changed, and with it the friction. Alex's cock felt longer inside me. Thicker. Hitting all the right spots. I pushed back, urging him to go faster.

He slapped my ass. "Stop moving."

"Make me."

His grip on my hair turned punishing, and he began thrusting inside me hard. Too hard. I planted my hands on the mattress and bucked against him. "You're hurting me."

He pulled out, and I expected him to say something, but he didn't. Instead, I felt strings of cool cum shooting on my lower back.

I dug my nails in his wrist until he let go of me. "What the fuck, Alex?"

"I'm sorry. I must have lost control. Are you all right?" He touched my shoulder gently.

I slapped his hand away and rolled onto my back, not caring if I stained the sheets. "No, I'm not fucking all right. What do you mean you lost control?" It was then I noticed his gaze was unfocused. He seemed stoned. "What happened?" I asked, worry threatening to dilute my anger.

"I don't know. I'm sorry. I thought I was dreaming. Didn't know I was really…"

"You were dreaming of using me as a sex toy?"

He cast his gaze down.

"Was it even me?" Or had he been fucking someone else? An insane stab of jealousy sliced through me.

"I don't know, all right?" His voice was high pitched, infused with a note of panic. "Did I hurt you badly?"

"I'll survive. Just don't let it happen again." It felt too little. I had to say more. He'd fucked me like I meant nothing to him. Like he didn't care if it was me or any other hole there for him to take his pleasure. He'd made me feel small. Insignificant.

I wasn't sure I wanted to tell him he had such power over me.

He nodded, black locks falling in front of his grey eyes and making him look like a lost puppy.

"I need to hit the shower." And think. I needed to think. Something was wrong with Alex, and I had to figure out what before it was too late. I wasn't afraid of him; he'd stopped the moment I'd said he was hurting me.

Or my pain had gotten him excited enough to come.

No. This wasn't—

"This isn't me," he said, echoing my thought.

I hoped it was the truth and this wasn't a side of him he'd kept hidden until now. But if it wasn't him, who was it? Did it have something to do with my turning him?

I got out of bed and took the sheets with me to the bathroom. Wesley did the laundry, but I could at least shove it into the hamper.

I turned the water on and adjusted it to room temperature before getting under the shower jet. Even with the roar of the water in my ears, I heard the door open. The next moment, Alex pulled the curtain out of the way and stepped in behind me.

"I'm sorry," he whispered in my ear. "I'm so sorry. I never wanted to hurt you, Cherry."

"I know."

His hands slid around to cup my breasts, then down my stomach, doing nothing more than caressing. "I'll spend the rest of eternity trying to make it up to you, I promise."

Logic dictated I shouldn't be feeling safe in the arms of a man who minutes ago was out of control, but this was Alex. I was safe with him. He was going through a rough patch. I'd been there too, freshly turned against my will and having to adjust to an entirely different existence.

I sighed and turned in his embrace. Shit happened. If that was the worst of it, we'd be okay. "You won't need to try for that long. The next ten to fifteen minutes should do."

"Yes, Ma'am." He kissed his way down my body and spent the rest of the shower on his knees.

By the time we came out, I was squeaky clean, thoroughly pleasured, and much less worried.

Until Alex told me to get dressed, because we were off to meet his mom in a little over an hour.

****

I wouldn't suggest meeting your boyfriend's mother for the first time *after* you've died. It's practically a given that she'll find you too pale, and your hand will be too cool to the touch.

Well aware of it, while getting ready to meet Alex's mom, I'd made sure to feed so I'd at least raise my temperature for a while—which isn't to say I didn't worry on the drive to her place. And all the way from her driveway to her front door.

"I should have worn something dressier." Alex had insisted my black skinny jeans and emerald-green silken blouse were perfect for a casual family dinner. At the time, I agreed. "Maybe we should reschedule?" I turned to look at Alex, who stood behind me as if to keep me from fleeing.

"Baby, I already rang the doorbell. Do you want us to make a run for it?" He tangled his fingers with mine and kissed the tip of my nose.

I opened my mouth to say *yes*, and then realized he wasn't being serious. "You're a meanie."

"Ah come on. You know you lo—Hey, Mom."

I swiveled around. The door was open, and a woman stood there studying us, a cheeky smile on her face. I liked her instantly. I'd seen pictures of her from fifteen or twenty years ago, but when Alex told me she was in her mid-sixties, I expected to see an old woman.

Mrs. Marsden appeared a decade or so younger than her real age. She was about my height, slim, and beautiful. She had Alex's midnight-black hair and steel-grey eyes, but I could see no other similarities between her and her son.

She wrapped her arms around Alex's neck, so she could plant a firm kiss on each of his cheeks. "About time you came to visit. I was arranging to take you off my will."

I winced. I was the one who'd delayed this visit.

Alex grinned. "You wouldn't do that. I'm the apple of your eye."

Mrs. Marsden turned to me. "See how he takes advantage of his poor old mother's love?"

Now was the time to say something smart. This was my only-chance-at-a-first-impression moment.

"Old?" I asked. "But I thought *you* were his mom." *Nailed it.*

"Oh, I knew I'd like you." She beamed at me. "I'm Sylvia. Come on in."

I smiled, a weight lifting off my shoulders. Yes, it was still scary meeting my boyfriend's mother, but she wasn't trying to make it harder for me. "I'm Cherry. And these are for you." I offered her the flowers we'd gotten for her.

She took the bouquet and pulled me in for a hug, which I wasn't prepared for. The flowers were squished between us. I caught my balance and returned her embrace awkwardly, hoping my breath didn't smell of blood.

"Come on in. I've made meatloaf." She looked at me. "You're not one of those vegetarian people, are you?"

"Far from it." Alex squeezed my hand. I squeezed back, and we shared a smile. If only she knew.

"I love meatloaf," I said, and we followed Sylvia inside.

I hadn't been to the Marsden residence since the day after Alex's turning, when he and I had cleaned up the evidence of his death. I expected to feel repulsion being back there—expected the stench of his life's blood to assault my nostrils.

I was in luck. The only memories that came back to me as we crossed his mother's living room were of our first nights together. Having incredible sex in the armchair and falling asleep, still linked. Alex's first realizing I was a vampire. Spending the day following Willoughby's attack in each other's arms.

I inhaled deeply, wanting to breathe in all the scents that made this house part of the man I loved.

Meatloaf was a nice addition to them.

"I hope you don't mind eating in the back yard," Sylvia said, leading the way through the kitchen. "It's such a lovely evening. You can see all the stars."

"That's a great idea." I clutched Alex's arm. The back yard was where we'd burned the sheets he'd bled out on, but it was okay, because he was still here. With me.

Sylvia had set the table with a checkered red tablecloth that reminded me of my own mom. What was it with me and memory lane tonight?

I focused on the meat, and saliva pooled in my mouth. "Sylvia, this smells divine."

She smiled. "Good. Sit, sit. Alex, I forgot the wine. Could you get it? It's by the sink."

I took a seat and watched as Sylvia piled two thick slices of meatloaf on my plate, topped them with gravy, and added mashed potatoes and salad on the side.

"Dig in," she said. "You could use a little extra weight."

Yeah, I loved her.

Alex served red wine and sat opposite me, leaving the seat at the head of the table for Sylvia, who slid in it gracefully.

I tried to be lady like and not overload my fork, but I wanted my first bite to have a bit of everything. And it did. It was perfect—juicy meat, creamy mashed potatoes, and crisp lettuce with the perfect balance of seasoning, olive oil, and balsamic. A little orgasm in my mouth.

Sylvia chose that exact moment to ask, "So, Cherry, Alex tells me you used to model. What do you do now?"

I'm not going to tell you the food lost its flavor, but it certainly turned dry enough to stick in my throat. I coughed and hit my chest with my fist.

"She's doing some private investigating, Ma. And she's good at it." Alex handed me my wine, and I downed it in one gulp. I'd done private investigating *once*, but his version of things sounded better than, 'She's an unemployed vampire.'

"Right. I forgot that's how you two met," Sylvia said.

From what Alex had said, I seriously doubted she was the sort of woman who'd forget anything. She was being a mom and trying to find out as much as she could about her son's girlfriend.

"Are you all right, Cherry?" Her voice was laced with concern.

"I'm fine. Couldn't resist stuffing my mouth, and it went down the wrong way. But yeah, P.I. is me. It doesn't pay that well, but I meet interesting people."

Alex preened, and Sylvia laughed. "Any exciting cases lately? My son used to keep me entertained with police stories. I sure hope his leave from work doesn't last much longer."

It probably would. I could see no way for Alex to return to the force and manage to keep his undead status a secret.

"I'm sorry to disappoint, but I'm on vacation too," I told Sylvia. And I planned to stay that way for as long as possible.

"Yeah, we decided to take the same time off. Get to know each other better," Alex added. He wasn't as happy about it as he pretended to be, but work-talk was something he'd been avoiding. I was glad to see it didn't bring him down now.

As a matter of fact, he seemed more at ease than I'd seen him in weeks. It warmed me up inside and confirmed my suspicions. In familiar settings, he was still himself. The newness of his situation was what caused his change in behavior. All we needed was time.

"Well, that sounds promising. Do I sense commitment in the near future? Maybe a grandchild, before I'm too old to help raise it?"

"*Mom.*" Alex gaped. I could see my blood rising on his cheeks.

"Oh, shush. Cherry can tell I'm not going to be pushy about it. Can't you, dear?" She didn't give me time to answer. "It's just that Alex has been badly hurt in the past, and—"

"I'm not planning on hurting him, Sylvia. *That* I can promise you." But only that. I couldn't promise her a grandchild. Ever. I'd taken that possibility away from Alex. Adoption was an option, in theory. But even if we decided to go that way and managed to compel a court into believing we were fit parents, how could we bring a child into our lives?

Sylvia patted my hand. My gaze found hers, and in it I saw all the worries of a single mother who wanted the best for her son. I wanted the best for him too, but I wasn't sure I knew what that was.

Alex broke the awkward silence. "You wanted to meet Cherry, so I brought her—knowing full well you'd embarrass me. When am I meeting Mr. O'Connor?"

Sylvia blushed.

"Mr. O'Connor?" I asked, arching an eyebrow. Alex had told me about him, but I felt like joining in his teasing of his mom.

"He is…" Sylvia didn't seem to know to know how to finish that sentence.

"He's Mom's boyfriend."

"That's so juvenile, Alex. Don't call him that." Sylvia made a moue of distaste.

"Okay. He's your gentleman caller. Your love interest?"

She gave him a light slap on the shoulder. "Cut that out. I get it. You want me out of your business, or you'll butt into mine. Mr. O'Connor and I are seeing each other. Taking things slowly."

"Not too slowly, I hope. You're not getting any younger."

"*Alex.*" Sylvia and I said in one voice.

"What? No brothers or sisters, before I'm too old to help raise them?"

Sylvia threw her hands up. "You're incorrigible. Eat while it's still warm, and I'll try to keep the discussion to harmless subjects. Like the weather. How do you like the weather, Cherry?"

"It's lovely," I said, "and so is the food."

Once we were done with the main course, Sylvia brought out a platter of pineapple upside-down cake, which Alex and I gleefully obliterated. By the time she walked us to the door, Alex carried a tinfoil packet with leftovers for the next day, and I was utterly taken with her.

She was so much like my mom, I couldn't help but give her a hug on my way out, careful not to put any strength to it. "Thank you so much, Sylvia. It was a pleasure meeting you." Out of the corner of my eye, I saw Alex sigh in relief.

"The pleasure was all mine, hon. Now try to keep him good, you hear? And if he gives you any trouble, call me."

I gave her another gentle squeeze, and then stepped back while she and Alex said goodnight.

"That wasn't all bad, was it?" Alex asked, as he backed the car out of his mom's driveway.

"Nope. Your mom kicks ass. I'm glad you insisted we come see her." Also, it was fun having some time away from the mansion and its drama.

"Told you she'd love you. And I'm sure your folks and I are going to hit it off."

Why did he have to go and remind me of that? Trepidation trailed cold fingers up my back. "You sure I can't change your mind about that trip?"

"Positive."

"I think I may try anyway."

The look he gave me was nowhere near playful. "Knock yourself out. I doubt it'll make a difference. We're off, as soon as Constantine says we can go."

"We'll see." I opened the window a bit and gulped down an unnecessary breath of fresh air, steeling myself for what I wanted to ask him. "Alex, is there anything you want to—you know, talk about?"

"Like what?"

"Like, about how you'll never be able to give your mom the grandchildren she wants?"

"Can't say I ever gave that a thought before, either."

"Yes, but then you could, if you wanted to. Now you're a vampire. A freak of nature. No beach outings for you. No tanning. No Sunday afternoon barbeques. And no babies in your future. You're not gonna get to be a daddy." I was sad to ruin the lovely evening we had, but I needed to hear he was okay with the decision I'd made for him.

"Cherry, let it go. Sun exposure is bad for humans too. And I don't know if I wanted to be a father anyway."

"But I took the choice away from y—"

He hit the steering wheel with both fists, hard enough to make one side of it bend visibly. "Will you stop saying that? I *had* no choice. I was dying. *Dead*. Now I'm here, because you saved me. I won't get into this with you again, so get over it. I'm *fine*."

I sat back and closed my eyes. If he was so *fine*, then what was with the outbursts? And why was he still refusing to drink human blood or have a serious discussion about permanently leaving the force? He wasn't fine. Not by a long shot. What I hated most was that I couldn't help him until he decided to open up. I could just be there for him and love him.

And introduce him to my parents.

Who'd spent the past six years thinking I was dead.

Fuck.

I tried to keep the thought at bay, but it still killed my good mood. When Alex asked if I felt like going for a drink, I told him I'd had an emotional day and would rather go straight home.

"Are you sure you're all right?" he asked when we reached the mansion. He pulled up to the entrance and tapped in the key code. The heavy steel gate slid open with a surprisingly faint sound, and we drove in.

"Yeah. I feel like spending the night in bed. Maybe I'll catch up on my reading."

Alex snorted.

"*Hey.* I do so read."

"Sure you do. So you won't mind if I leave you alone? I owe Constantine a rematch."

"You never told me why things were so tense last night," I said casually.

"I'm a sore loser. You know that." His chuckle sounded forced.

"I know. I just don't want there to be any bad blood between you and him."

"We're fine."

That was obviously all I'd get out of him on the subject. Maybe Alex wasn't the one to ask what had transpired. Good thing he wasn't the only one who knew the truth.

We walked to our room holding hands. It felt nice. I watched him put on his sweats and kissed him for good luck before he left to find Constantine.

Then I kicked off my high-heeled booties and flopped on the bed. I switched on the forty-two inch TV that hung on the wall across from me and let my mind be lulled by what passes for entertainment these days.

Chapter Five

Vampire hearing is about a hundred times more acute than human is. As with our sight, we're lucky we can regulate it, or we'd run the risk of bleeding eardrums.

Like, for instance, when a piercing screech and the banging of a door reverberated through the entire floor.

I jumped up and rushed out of the room, letting the ongoing cries lead me. Was it Sheena? Had something happened to her?

Had one of the vampettes snapped and attacked her for blood? Constantine was supposed to keep them in check. I rounded the corner to his room and saw Liza banging on the closed door.

"Sally, come out, and we'll talk about it," she said.

Nothing but wailing from the other side.

"What happened?" I asked.

Liza slammed her open palm on the door. "*Sally.* Don't make me break down the door. I doubt Constantine will appreciate the mess."

I wasn't surprised when she ignored me. Before we saved the girls from Willoughby and his cohorts, he'd convinced them I wanted to destroy them. Though they'd come to realize he was a creepy liar and a killer, and they no longer screeched in fear every time they saw me, they still didn't hold me in the highest regard.

Carrie leaned against the wall behind Liza, shaking her head. Her dark chocolate-brown hair was swept into a loose bun. I much preferred this hairdo to the Ádísa-inspired braid she used to sport. Carrie might still be a little wary of me, but at least she no longer idolized the woman responsible for her and her friends' deaths.

"What's wrong?" I asked her.

"Sally is being a brat." She rolled her eyes, but her full mouth was drawn in a thin line. She was worried. She and Liza were always protective of Sally, who was the most innocent and doe eyed of the three.

Liza turned to me now. "We were watching one of those makeover shows, and she flipped out. She doesn't want to be a vampire any longer."

"I don't," came Sally's voice from the other side of the door. "I'd rather die."

"Well, you can't do that in there, honey. There's no way to."

"I'll starve myself," Sally yelled.

"Get Constantine," I mouthed to Carrie, who nodded and took off toward the gym. To Sally, I said, "That will take a long time, and you know we'll get you out before then."

Liza glared. "Are you telling her to find a faster way to off herself?"

Was that what I'd done? I don't always do well under pressure. "Okay, don't open the door," I said to Sally. "Just listen to me for a few, yes? None of us wanted this. I don't know about Constantine, but nobody asked me if I wanted to die and become an undead chick, who can never drop a pound. Alex was brutally attacked and left for dead in his parents' house. I loved him too much to let him go, but I'm still not sure I did well to force this existence on him."

My voice broke, but I went on. "What happened to you was wrong and unfair, and I swear Willoughby will pay for it. He'll pay for what he did to all of us. But there are perks too, and you need to focus on them. Can you do that? Sally?" I listened, but only muffled sobs reached my ears. "Maybe we should break the door," I said and rattled the knob.

"Maybe you shouldn't." Constantine's voice came from right behind me. I turned and bumped into his very naked chest. Why did he and Alex have to spar topless?

Great. Now I had mental images of the two of them wrestling, glistening torsos rubbing together.

Of course, there was no sweat trickling down Constantine's pale abs. Vampires don't perspire. We drool, though, and I had to check myself, to make sure I wasn't doing just that. "Where is Alex?" My voice was cool. As cool as his skin, *that I was still touching.*

I looked up and met his gaze. His expression was flat, but there was a twinkle of mirth in his eyes. "He's doing his stretches, hoping he'll fall to the floor more elegantly next time I throw him across the room," he said.

My thoughts shifted to the way more appropriate image of Alex stretching, muscles rippling along the tan skin of his chest and back. Yum. Constantine and his state of undress no longer frazzled me. I'd just been caught off guard.

"Can you talk her out of there?" I pointed at the door.

Constantine nodded. "Sally? Can you please come out? I want to help you, but I can't, unless you let me know what's wrong." His voice was honey sweet and thick and intimate.

He spoke to me in that lover's voice a long time ago, but I never before heard him use it on any of the girls. I didn't know what happened between them behind the closed doors of his bedroom, but in my presence, he treated them more like beloved nieces. Though there was no mistaking the lusty looks the three gave him, all he seemed genuinely interested in was their well being.

Hearing him urge to Sally to talk to him, I realized he enjoyed more than their company. Did they all share his bed at the same time, or did they take turns?

So *not* something I wanted to dwell on.

"Sally, please open the door. You know I only want what's best for you, baby," Constantine said.

It felt weird hearing him call someone else baby, but there was no stab of jealousy. Good. My subconscious was catching up to reality.

Sally threw open the door and literally flew into his waiting arms. "We'll fix everything," he whispered into her hair.

We all heard.

"Maybe the rest of you ladies should give us some privacy?" Constantine said.

I reluctantly followed Carrie and Liza down the corridor.

"You coming upstairs?" Liza asked. "We got Wesley to order us chicken nuggets. You don't wanna miss his face when we dig in. The man prefers watching us drink blood than eat junk food."

Ruffling Wesley's feathers was always fun. The old human was always the epitome of decorum, though he had his naughty side. More than I liked the idea of witnessing his horror at our culinary faux pas, I was happy Liza wanted to include me. Maybe I was slowly becoming part of their group. It'd be good not to have to deal with their resentment while we shared a roof, and to be honest, I kind of liked them.

I smiled. "Sounds good, but maybe later. We just got back from a kickass meatloaf dinner."

She nodded. "Later."

Carrie threw me a finger wave over her shoulder, and they took the stairs up, while I headed for my room.

****

I'd changed into shorts and a T-shirt, when there was a knock on the door.

"It's open," I said, wondering why Alex would bother knocking.

Constantine poked his head in. "May I come in?"

"Sure." I had on more than I usually wore to bed, but I didn't want Alex to find me naked when he turned in for the day. Sally had seemed perfectly all right until her breakdown, and wondering if Alex was going down the same path put me off the mood for sexy times.

"Damn. You're dressed." Constantine pushed the door open all the way and sauntered inside, stopping by the foot of the bed. Lean and wiry, graceful and light-footed, he reminded me of a jungle cat zeroing in on its prey.

He only had his sweatpants on, and the way they hung low on his hips revealed there was nothing underneath but smooth, pale skin.

It was annoying how good he looked. I mean, I shared a bed with a gorgeous, chiseled man, who usually didn't bother with clothes around me, yet Constantine's body was nothing short of a work of art. Each curve, each angle, each line seemed perfectly thought of in advance, as though by a sculptor set out to carve the flawless male specimen.

And his every step showed he knew that.

Eh, at least he no longer frazzled me.

"How's Sally?" I asked.

"Better. I reminded her of some of the pros of being a vampire."

"Like stamina in bed?" My grin was genuine.

"No, you wicked creature. Like how she will never have to worry about wrinkles." He scratched his chest in a manner that was too sexy not to have been rehearsed. "This isn't why I called on you, though. I wanted to let you know we're leaving as soon as you're packed tomorrow evening. Alex is driving us, and I've arranged for supplies. Pack light, will you?"

I nodded. "Is this really a smart idea?"

"Packing light?"

"Stop acting obtuse—we both know you're not. If I do need to spell it out for you, though, do you believe visiting my parents is the right thing to do?"

He stepped closer and sat on the edge of the mattress, by my side. "I know this must be scary for you, but it's clearly important to Alex. If you don't think you can handle it, you only have to say the word. I'll tell him I changed my mind and won't allow it. But if you want to see your family again, and all that's holding you back is fear, I have your back."

"I know." A tightness grew in my chest, where my heart no longer beat.

"Perchance 'thank you' would be a more appropriate response? 'I don't know what I'd do without you' might also work."

"Yeah, yeah, you rock." I tugged at the end of his ponytail, the tightness giving way only slightly.

Constantine was the only vampire I knew whose irises changed color according to his mood. When they were the dark blue of the winter sea, I felt like he could see right through me. Now he narrowed his eyes and gave me that look from which I knew I couldn't hide. "We're going, then?"

"We're going."

"And you're happy with Alex?"

The question startled me. "Well, that was out of left field. Why wouldn't I be?"

"Just checking."

"Has he said anything to you? Is that what the thing last night was about? Sheena said the two of you were ready to go for each other's throat."

"That was nothing. Boys being boys."

"When the boys have the strength of bulldozers, it's not exactly nothing."

"He was setting his boundaries. It's inevitable in situations where two dominant males share the same space."

"So you don't think he's unhappy and lashing out?"

"He's not the one I care about." His irises swam with different shades of blue. I'd never seen them do that before.

"Constantine, don't…" What? Don't care about me? I'd already asked him not to, especially after the way things ended between us. It didn't seem to work.

He shook his head. "It's not something he said. He seems on edge. Constantly alert—ready for war, even."

"It's the cop in him."

"No, it's more than that. It's as if he knows something's coming, but doesn't know when to expect it."

"What's coming? What do you mean?"

He sighed. "I make no sense, even to myself. Ignore me."

Yeah, *that* would be easy. "I can't keep on ignoring things, Constantine. I've tried to wait out Alex's issues, because his world just turned upside down, but you don't have that excuse. Tell me what's coming."

He closed his eyes. When he opened them again, the swirl of emotion was gone. "I don't know. I swear. Alex seems to, however, and he's preparing for it."

There was the frozen fist clenching around my heart again. "I don't know what to do, how to help him. He says he's fine, everything is fucking *fine*, but I can see that's a lie. He won't feed except from me; he won't officially leave the force. It's as if he's trying to convince himself nothing's changed. Like he believes being a vampire is a phase, and he'll eventually outgrow it. I can't explain it any better."

"It must be his defense mechanism—how he's dealing with this transition. You know it's too big a change for someone to accept all once." His voice was soft, and I wished I could tell him how much his reassurances meant to me without leading him on.

"You're probably right."

"As is usually the case."

I smiled. "Wisdom comes with great age, after all."

"Yes, yes, I'm ancient. Ha-ha." He sobered. "Will you be all right?"

"Yup."

"And lightly packed by dusk tomorrow?"

"I'll try."

"Good." He kissed me on the forehead and stood. "Alex will be here as soon as he's done licking his wounds. I'm ashamed to say I wiped the floor with him."

"You're so not ashamed to say so."

"You're absolutely right." He gave me that bone-jellifying smirk of his, but something was lacking. Despite his smart-mouthed responses, his whole demeanor seemed more subdued than usual.

He was at the door, when I asked, "What are you keeping from me?"

"Nothing to do with Alex, I assure you."

Chapter Six

Alex was all smiles when he came back. Given Constantine had kicked his ass, his cheerfulness was surprising, until I realized Alex had to already know we were leaving in less than twenty-four hours. Part of me begrudged him for insisting on meeting my parents after I'd told him how awkward it would be for me. Another part was grateful I'd get to at least give them some closure. Those two parts fighting brought me as close to a migraine, as vampiricaly possible.

I watched Alex throw clothes into a duffel bag and tried to focus on how the muscles in his arms and back bunched and relaxed every time he bent over, and how his sweatpants stretched over his ass.

Even then, my mood wouldn't improve. "Can you at least stop whistling?" I asked.

"I'm sorry; I didn't realize I was." He seemed sincere enough, so I bit down on a bitter comment about his being off key.

"It's okay. I'm just antsy about tomorrow. I don't see any possible scenario, in which my parents don't freak out and call an exorcist, if we tell them the truth."

"We don't have to tell them everything, Cherry. All they need to know is that you're still around, seeing a great guy"—he made a sweeping gesture, encompassing himself head to toe—"and that you're happy. Any parent would be ecstatic to know their child is well and happy."

"Never mind that said child dropped off the face of the Earth for six years," I muttered.

"There are ways of explaining that. A drug problem, a cult, a spy career—"

"You're hilarious." Despite my sarcastic reply, I could feel a smile tugging at the corners of my mouth.

"Then wait till you hear my best idea yet." He mimicked the sound of a drum rolling. "You ready?"

"Doubt it."

"Alien abduction. How's that?"

"Brilliant. It might land me in the loony bin faster than the truth would."

He laughed and pulled me close for a kiss. His lips, soft against mine, were as effective in melting away some of my worry as his words were. "We'll figure it out. We'll figure it *all* out. Don't worry."

"Constantine said the same thing."

Alex stiffened, but only for a moment. "See? With us two, you have nothing to fear."

Yeah. Nothing. Except for the moment they turned on each other. "As long as you both play nice, I couldn't ask for better allies." I buried my face between his neck and shoulder, and let my fangs graze his skin. It was my way of showing him I wanted him, even in the midst of all the crazy.

"As long as you're in my bed, I've no reason to be anything *but* nice." I could tell he didn't mean it as a threat, but something in his tone rang a warning bell.

"And if I'm no longer in your bed?"

In lieu of an answer, Alex picked me up, shoved me against the wall, and wedged his hips between my thighs. When I opened my mouth to protest, he closed his lips over mine. It was nothing like his previous effort to reassure me. No soft pressing of lips—rather, sharp teeth and probing tongue. The hunger he poured into the kiss was frightening in its intensity. If I had a breath, he would have stolen it away.

He ground his erection against my mound and kneaded my buttocks with his palms. "Never gonna happen. You're mine forever," he said when he finally pulled back.

Lightheaded, I found my footing and straightened my shorts. I…didn't really have an answer to that. It sounded romantic, something a lover was supposed to say, but felt more primal than I was comfortable with. I forced myself to smile. "Let's finish packing. Before we start planning forever, we have to make it through the next few days."

"We will. You'll see. Your parents will be thrilled, and they're going to love me. And once we have their blessings, maybe we could move things forward. Make sure our relationship is going somewhere. There's no reason for us not to have a life, just because we're dead."

He was obviously in Lala-land.

When Constantine had been my sponsor—a sort of mentor the now defunct Vampire Social Services assigned to fledglings—he'd kept telling me eternity would make me see things differently. For the first time, I clearly got what that meant. Vampires aren't *people*-people. Our dietary needs aren't the only thing telling us apart from humans. Alex still didn't understand that. He thought we could play house indefinitely.

And I was burdened with the responsibility to show the man I loved that his life had changed a great deal more than he realized.

Sadness filled my heart. Had I lost too much of my humanity, or was Alex trying too hard to hold onto his? Instead of lingering on that and slamming reality in his face, I allowed him to pull me into his fantasy, where we moved into our own little place and got a dog and made friends with the neighbors. It was a beautiful daydream. Alex's eyes sparkled with more life than I'd seen in them since the night of his turning, and when he laughed at our imaginary dog's imaginary antics, I found myself joining him.

By dawn, my worries were at the back of my mind. We got into bed, and Alex cuddled me from behind. There was nothing sexual about his embrace. He held me, and I drifted off feeling safe and happy.

Until a deep growl snapped me fully awake.

I rolled to face Alex, but he was faster, pulling my body beneath his and pinning me to the bed.

I thought he was going for some kink, until I met his gaze. His eyes looked vacant. He dug one of his hands into the soft flesh of my stomach and squeezed my windpipe with the other. *Oh, God.* There was a monster holding me down, wearing my lover's face.

I clawed at his hand, raising bloody welts on the skin, but he wouldn't let go. Panic rose inside me. I was in no danger from lack of oxygen, but the way he balanced his weight on me was beyond painful.

I tried to call his name, wake him up—he *had* to be asleep; it *had* to be a nightmare; this wasn't my Alex—but could manage nothing more than a whisper.

I couldn't talk to him.

I couldn't scream for help.

Now that he too was a vampire, he outmatched me in physical strength like a two hundred and ten pound human man outmatched a hundred and thirty pound human woman. I could possibly toss him to the ground in a karate match, but couldn't fight him off when he already held me down. I kept trying to buck him off me anyway. Tears welled in my eyes, and sensory memory convinced me my legs had gone numb, though I rationally knew it wasn't possible for a vampire.

"Alex," I mouthed, "please."

I don't know if it was my silent plea or something else, but his weight was suddenly off me. He disappeared so fast, I couldn't follow him with my gaze. I heard the bathroom door slam shut. His voice came muffled from the other side. "Nightmare. What the fuck…? This isn't me. This isn't me. *This isn't me.*"

The desperation in his voice scared me more than his attack had.

I didn't know what to do. I wanted to put as much distance between us as possible, but the daylight held me captive in the basement, and I wasn't going to seek refuge in Constantine's room.

I didn't need to run or hide. Alex wouldn't attack me when he was fully conscious. He had a nightmare and fought back, not knowing it was me.

But my throat still hurt from his grip.

The water stopped running in the shower and another hour passed, before I realized Alex wasn't coming back anytime soon. I kept telling myself I was in no danger if he returned, but I couldn't relax. The thought of him getting back into bed while I was asleep sent a jolt of fear to my very core and kept me awake.

I couldn't be afraid of my lover. He never wanted to hurt me. It wasn't him.

Whatever his nightmares were about, they were messing with his head and they were messing with me. I thought of going to him and forcing him to come clean, but I was too much of a coward to confront him. Besides, I was sure I knew what he was dreaming of. It was his violent turning. Lying in his childhood bed. Bleeding to death.

All because he'd met me.

I didn't want him to talk about it, because I didn't want to hear him blame me.

I busied myself, unpacking and repacking our bags for the trip. Most of Alex's t-shirts were in dire need of better folding anyway. Being surrounded by his clothes, by his scent, gradually mellowed me out.

When he finally left the bathroom, the sun was down. He smelled of shower gel and deo, his hair was tousled to perfection, and his smile was wide. It was like nothing had happened.

He shouldered both our bags and held out a hand. The same hand that had hurt me. "Shall we?" His gaze was pleading.

I remembered him leading me out of *The Gridlock* the first time we met, his palm on the small of my back. His touch always made me feel safe, even when he was a human and physically weaker than me, and his long fingers gave me pleasure countless times.

I was beyond pissed that he'd pretend nothing had happened. I wanted him to come clean about his nightmares—or night-terrors, or whatever the hell he saw in his sleep that turned him into a savage animal. I wanted to smack some sense into him.

But I refused to fear his hand.

Promising myself I'd confront him as soon as we returned from our trip, I nodded and placed my palm in his. "We shall."

Chapter Seven

"But what if something comes up I can't handle? Sally may have another breakdown." Liza's voice was reasonable, but her gaze betrayed her worry.

I winced, the memory of Sally's sobs still fresh in my memory. Liza wasn't sure she'd remain focused on the perks of her newly acquired vampirism. To be honest, neither was I.

"Sally will be all right, and you'll have Sheena and Wesley here to help you. I'm sure you won't require any assistance, though. You're as capable of maintaining balance in the manor as I am." Constantine trailed his index finger down the perfect slope of her cheekbone and leaned down to place a lingering kiss on her lips. I'm pretty sure she sniffled when he broke away.

I averted my gaze, not wanting to intrude. It was odd, waiting outside the front door with Alex, while Constantine locked lips with all three young vampires. Wesley wrapped his arms around Carrie and Sally, and Sheena touched Liza lightly on the shoulder.

"It's okay. They'll be back soon," Sheena said.

Liza nodded and looked at me. "Call when you get there."

"Will do." I smiled. Our forced cohabitation was evolving into a tentative friendship, and I liked it.

Don't know how I'd feel if it were my house we'd all camped in, but Constantine didn't seem to mind the company. That wasn't the case from the beginning. When I'd sneaked Sheena to his place, to save her from Willoughby, Constantine had found her insufferable. He wasn't exactly thrilled when I'd volunteered him to take in the three fledglings either. Still, he'd offered Alex and me a place too, when we needed to lie low.

Of course, now he had a steady supply of lovers who didn't demand exclusivity, a verbal sparring partner in Sheena, an actual sparring partner in Alex, and… me. I wasn't sure where I fit in, but I was in no hurry to find out.

If anyone was to be bothered by the new living arrangements, it should be Wesley, who took care of everything and everyone, but he'd repeatedly commented on how brilliant it was having new blood—of sorts—enter the mansion.

Goodbyes exchanged, the three of us hopped in Alex's Chrysler. I rode shotgun, while Constantine made himself comfortable, sprawled in the back seat.

"Anybody feel like a snack?" he asked, tapping the portable fridge next to him.

"Cherry's brought her own," Alex said. "I'm pretty sure she emptied the kitchen cabinets on the way out."

"Someone's in a good mood," I muttered. It was going to be a delightful four-hour ride to San Luis Obispo.

Not.

Halfway there—about fifty miles from Santa Barbara—I was hungry for blood, on edge, and sick of Alex's running commentary on the scenic coastal route. He wasn't our damned tour guide. He and I weren't at a chit-chatty place. I didn't know what place we were at, but it felt cold and lonely. I was about to reach out and smack him in the mouth, when I caught Constantine's gaze in the rearview mirror. His face looked drawn, but the understanding in his tired eyes shocked me.

He gave me a tight smile and leaned his head against the window. "Alex, can you please shut up about the plunging mountain line and put some decent music on? We'll have enough talking to do when we get there."

Instead of snapping at him, Alex grinned and put on a CD. "Forgot you were probably around when the coastline formed, grandpa."

Constantine gave him a one-finger salute through the mirror, and rock music filled the car. I knew the song, but didn't lip-sync to it, like I usually did to protect the innocent from my vocal grandeur. Instead, I let it act as white noise, allowing me time with my thoughts. And my worries.

I had gone along with the men's plan because I loved Alex and wanted to do this for him. And I really loved the thought of seeing my parents again, after so long. On the ride, we came up with an amnesia story for why I'd fallen off the face of the earth for half a dozen years, but I wasn't entirely satisfied with it. It didn't explain why I didn't go to the police, who'd have matched me to my missing-person file, or why I wouldn't be able to visit during the day.

Right now, the best case scenario in my head had my parents ignoring my excuses, thinking I'd been kidnapped and brainwashed, and calling the police on Constantine and Alex.

Why had I waited this long to go back to them? Why had I followed the council's stupid rules? They were my parents. They loved me. Even if I told them the truth, they'd accept me.

Would they?

"It's all going to be fine," Alex said and let go of the gear shift to take my hand. "They'll be ecstatic to see you. Stick with the amnesia angle, and we'll be fine."

"If I hear the word fine one more time, I may scream." I shook off his grip.

"It'll be great. Wonderful. Amazing."

I snorted. Sure it would. I'd say, "Mom, Dad, I'm alive. I was in an accident that nobody heard anything about, then had amnesia, and now I'm here in the middle of the night, to introduce you to my boyfriend and my ex—who really has no valid reason for being here." Mom and Dad would hug me, and we'd all rejoice.

I sighed and let my head fall back.

Constantine closed his large palm on my shoulder. "We'll figure it all out. You deserve that."

Where was the snark? Where was the jackass, who cheated on me and tried to pass it off as natural for our kind? Or the pain in my butt, who had a comment about everything I said or did under his roof?

Why couldn't Alex and Constantine settle in their respective roles as doting boyfriend and calculating former lover, and stop messing with my head?

Because life would be way too easy, if they did.

"Either of you feel like a snack?" Alex asked.

"Not hungry," I said. I was famished, but we might as well get it over with.

"What about you, Cee? Care to sample the locals?"

Now they were on a nickname basis, and Alex was joking about feeding on humans? I wasn't sure I'd be able to wait till we were back to confront him.

"Nah. I'll bag it," Constantine said.

I turned to look at him over my shoulder, brow furrowed. "What did you say?"

He shrugged and pulled a blood bag out of the mini-fridge. "My new protégés come with an entirely new vocabulary. I grow old ever learning many things."

Protégés.

Not sex kittens.

Right.

Alex said something that sounded like 'soul on.'

"Huh?"

Whatever explanation he gave went unheard. I was too busy wondering why it bugged me that while Constantine and I had been together, I'd been the only one doing any learning.

****

It was well after midnight, by the time reached my home town.

"Can you give me directions to our hotel, or should I look it up?" Alex held up his phone.

"I know how to get us there," I said. "I… Maybe we should go straight to my parents' place?" Now we were close, I was getting antsy. I needed to see them. See they were okay. See their reaction when they realized I was back.

Feel their love.

For the four years since Constantine and I broke up, and until fate threw Alex my way, I'd been alone. My only concern had been to make it another day. Find another guy to feed on. Compel someone to cover my rent. It was a routine I'd gotten used to, and found hard to leave behind, when Alex barged in my life demanding truth and feelings and commitment.

Now I accepted there could be more to my unlife than eternally smooth skin. I had a man who loved me, friends, and a kickass place to call home.

I needed to know if I could also have my family.

"I can't say this is the best time for a visit," Constantine said. "We could unpack, maybe feed, and wait until sundown tomorrow?"

I shook my head. "If we don't go now, I'm not sure I can go at all." Anticipation and fear rolled inside my stomach in a jumble.

"Cold feet?" Alex squeezed my thigh.

I chuckled, no longer caring he'd been an ass. His touch reassured me. "That's putting it mildly."

"Lead the way, then."

I did. I gave him instructions all the way to the house I'd grown up in.

For the latter part of our trip, all I'd heard had been the growling of my stomach, but I forgot all about my hunger when I saw the freshly paved driveway. I'd walked, skipped, and sneaked along this driveway so many times.

We parked and got out of the car. The moment Alex slammed his door shut, a small light appeared on the first floor of the house, where my parents' bedroom window faced the street. My night vision kicked in when a dark shape formed behind the curtain. My mother stood there, and I could tell she looked our way.

I ran my fingers along the collar of my shirt. Maybe I should have worn something less casual than a shirt and jeans. Would Mom approve of my new hair? She always liked its natural blond, and this red was too fake.

Stupid thought to have. She wouldn't notice the hair. Her only daughter was home.

More lights came on. I rushed to the front door forcing myself to only use human speed. Alex fell back a couple steps, allowing me some space, but Constantine caught up with me and grabbed my forearm as I reached for the doorbell. I'd psyched myself enough to go through with it, and he cut me off.

I let my annoyance show on my face. "Seriously?"

"There's something you should know," he said, apparently unfazed by my glare. "I made a promise a long time ago. I tried to figure a way around it, but I couldn't break it."

"Just spit it out, please. Better yet, save it for later."

It was as though he didn't hear me. "Anyway, I haven't known for long, either. Only found out a week ago. After I joined the council, I did some digging. It wasn't easy. There was essentially no digital footprint."

Alex cleared his throat. We both turned to look at him. "You're rambling," he told Constantine. Constantine never rambled.

"I know. The thing is, it wasn't my choice to—" Before Constantine could finish his sentence, the door was thrown open to reveal my mom. Her hair was pulled back in the high, untidy bun she always favored. There were thin lines around her light brown eyes, and her roots showed her hair was really mostly grey under the chestnut dye, but other than that, she looked like I remembered.

My mouth went dry. What could I say? Hi? Greetings, human? Or maybe, I missed you?

I'm sorry?

I wouldn't be able to set foot in my family home without being invited in; my name wasn't in the deeds.

I stood there staring at my mother, my lips moving but not forming words.

She smiled, and her face lit up. "What took you so long?" she asked. I barely had time to register her lack of surprise, before she threw her arms around me and pulled me into a tight hug. Too soon, she withdrew and held me at arm's length. "You've lost weight. Looks good."

What the fuck? She hadn't seen me or heard from me in years, and that was the first thing she said?

I opened my mouth to voice my thoughts, but Mom let go of me and gave Constantine a kiss on the cheek. "I didn't dare contact you, after everything. Should have known you'd find her and bring her home."

Huh? I exchanged a perplexed look with Alex. At least someone looked more confused than I felt.

Constantine ducked his head like a shy school boy. "I'm so sorry, Kathleen," he said. "I didn't know she was your daughter until last week. I should have seen the resemblance, but the eyes threw me." The words were whispered, but I heard them loud and clear.

Was that the night of a million surprises?

"Yeah, she's got Greg's coloring," my mom supplied as coolly as if she were talking about the weather.

"Um, excuse me?" I lifted my hand in the air. "How do you two know each other?" What was happening? My ex and my mom seemed perfectly at ease around each other, like old friends. They better not have been anything more, or…

Yuck. I shook off the thought and focused on something else. If my mom had known Constantine for a while, she had to have noticed he didn't age.

"Is it—" Dad showed up behind Mom, pulling his robe on over his pajamas. His eyes lit up when his gaze landed on me. "It is you. Finally. Welcome home, Princess. Let me look at you. You're so beautiful. God, I've missed you." He tied his robe's sash, wrapped his arms around my waist, and twirled me in the air, like he used to when I was a little girl. "Ruby said you'd come back. Your mother was sure, but I missed you."

I was too shocked to ask what my mom's younger sister, Ruby, had to do with it all. I gave my dad a gentle squeeze, trying not to think of how I could twirl him far easier than he could me. "I missed you too. Lots."

"She's here now, hon." Mom patted his shoulder. "Come in, everyone."

She moved toward the kitchen, and I rushed after her. "What about you? Did you miss me?"

Someone—probably Alex—rested a calming hand on my back. I stepped out of reach. I didn't want to be calm.

My mom swiveled around, eyebrows arched. "Of course I missed you, sweetie. Why would you think otherwise?"

"Oh, I don't know. You haven't seen me in six years, and all I get is, 'Hi. Took you long enough. Yay, weight loss?' Don't you fucking care I'm back?" I felt like crying. For years I'd hated being unable to let them know I was still around. I worried they'd be devastated by my disappearance, and now she acted like I'd been on a planned vacation.

She gathered me close and kissed me on the forehead. "I care more than you'll ever know. I waited up for you every single night since your disappearance." I tensed before giving in. She still smelled like apples, cookies, and fabric softener, only a million times more intensely than she used to.

She smelled like home.

Unshed tears shone in her eyes, and I finally saw what my disappearance had cost her. "There's so much we need to talk about," she said. "We missed you like crazy, but we always knew you were all right. Let me get you all something to drink, and we'll explain everything." She gave me one of her trademark glares. "And mind your manners. No more using the f-word while you're under our roof; I didn't raise a punk."

I nodded and turned to the table, needing some space to compose myself. My gaze fell on Alex. He leaned against the kitchen wall, stiller than I'd never seen him before, and as obscure as his large frame allowed. I linked my arm through his and pulled him forward to stand by my side, happy when the dejected look slid off his face.

At the same time, my dad held out his hand. "We all seem to have forgotten our manners tonight. I'm Greg. My wife's Kathleen. Any friend of Gerri's or Constantine's is a friend of ours."

Constantine let out a low chuckle at the sound of my human nickname. I narrowed my eyes at him, and he gave me a wicked smirk.

Alex took Dad's proffered hand. "Alex. Nice to meet you." Not like he was surprised to hear what I was really called; he'd found my missing person report file, including all my personal info, the day after we'd first met.

Constantine made himself comfortable at the table. "Alex is Cherry's boyfriend. I have wanted to tell her everything since I found out, but couldn't until I contacted you. And of course your number isn't registered. When Alex insisted we visit you, I seized the opportunity to have you explain."

"Cherry?" My dad arched both eyebrows.

"It's what Gertrude goes by these days," Constantine said, before I could speak.

I wasn't little Gertrude Mosby any longer—hadn't been in a long while—and my new name was only one in a list of changes I'd have to fill my parents in on.

"I'll explain," I said, "but later. First, Mom, how did you… How do you know Con—"

Mom turned from the fridge, and the words died in my mouth, as I saw what was in her hand.

Three bags of blood.

I felt my jaw drop. "What's that?"

"Judging by the time, I guess…brunch." She looked at Alex. "You are like them, right?"

"I don't really…" Alex seemed at a total loss, which funnily was exactly how I felt.

"Alex is new. He isn't yet comfortable with our ways," Constantine said. "Your mother knows," he told me. "She and your father both."

No shit.

"I can't believe you didn't tell me you knew them," I hissed at him. "I thought you were done hiding things."

"I didn't hide it. I couldn't tell you."

"Don't blame Constantine. He promised to not tell a soul we know about your kind, and he's a man of his word," Dad said.

So yelling at my ex would have to wait. First I had to figure out if he'd compelled my parents into thinking him trustworthy.

Mom popped the bags in the microwave oven and set it for half a minute, before placing three mugs on the counter. "How about some tea, then?" she asked Alex.

"That would be great. Lots of sugar, please."

I let go of him and ran both hands over my face. "Okay, this is too weird for me. How did you know about me? About us, in general?"

Dad pulled out chairs for us all, and Mom handed us the filled mugs. "I'll tell you everything. Sit. Drink." She fleetingly caressed my cheek, her touch tender as ever, grounding me.

I took a seat and cupped my drink with both hands. I didn't know what I'd hear, but my world would never be the same again. Hell, it had already changed. I'd just found out I'd wasted years I could have spent with my family, for no reason. They knew what I was. I wanted to blame Constantine for it, but I believed he hadn't known sooner.

Alex sat next to me and placed a hand on my shoulder. I rubbed my cheek against his knuckles and steeled myself for whatever truth was coming my way.

Chapter Eight

"I—I don't know where to start." Mom gave us a watery smile.

"Try the beginning." Dad winked at her, and they shared a look that made me happy deep inside. Whatever else had changed, my parents were still as perfect a couple as I remembered them being.

She nodded. "When I was five, back in Ireland—"

I frowned. "In Ireland?"

"Yes, I grew up there."

"How come I never heard of that?"

"Really not what you should be focusing on, honey." Mom shook her head. "A month after my fifth birthday, to be exact, my mother and I were attacked on our way home from visiting a friend. My mother shoved me behind her and begged our attacker not to harm me. The woman completely ignored me, but went straight for my mother's neck. It was after sundown. I remember her opening her mouth, and her canines gleaming in the moonlight, long as my pinky. And I remember my mom collapsing and blood spurting on my good dress."

"A vampire?" I whispered.

"Not just any vampire," said Constantine. "It was Ádísa."

"You know her?" Mom asked me. She looked horrified.

"I did, Mom. She was… She had me turned." Mom gasped, and I clasped her hand. "She can't hurt any of us anymore. Constantine took care of her for good."

Tears shone in her eyes, and she mouthed a silent thank you to him.

Constantine shook his head, as if killing his maker was nothing worth mentioning. "She was set on having your grandfather as her consort," he said to me. "When he wouldn't cheat on his wife with her, Ádísa decided to simply eliminate the competition. My maker always was a sore loser."

That was unbelievable. "Ádísa was after Grandpa Geoffrey?" And Grandma Ross had won? I cheered inwardly for the woman I'd never met.

"She had already tried to seduce him, but he wouldn't leave us," Mom said. "I never found out whether he briefly gave into her advances or not. My mother never said. Maybe she didn't know. Anyway, Constantine witnessed the attack and heard your grandma cry that she didn't want to leave her baby girl—me—an orphan. He…"

"I turned her," Constantine said flatly. "I was no innocent. I'd done my share of indiscriminate killing, both as a human and as a vampire, but she… I couldn't let her die on the side of the road, covered in dirt, with her toddler watching."

"You turned Cherry's grandmother?" Alex sounded both incredulous and furious. I covered his palm with mine, and he sat back, but he was obviously still on edge.

"My grandma was a vampire? And you were her maker? Why didn't I know this sooner?"

"I told you"—Constantine sounded impatient—"I had no idea you were her granddaughter. I didn't recognize your family name."

"But you knew my dad. You must have known his last name."

"Listen to the whole story, and you'll understand," Mom said. "The important thing is he saved her."

I stared at Constantine. He returned my gaze, unfazed by my scrutiny. Every time I thought I had the man figured out, he showed me another side of himself. As he'd done a couple months back, when I thought he'd betrayed me for Ádísa, only to watch him behead her—his own *maker*—to save Alex and me.

Or maybe he wasn't all that chivalrous, and my grandma had been even better looking than Mom told me. Aunt Ruby was supposed to look a lot like her.

"Hold on." I looked at my mother. "What about aunt Ruby? How was she born? She's almost six years younger than you. Was grandma pregnant when Constantine turned her? But then she couldn't have— How…?"

Mom and Constantine exchanged a look. To me, she said, "Stop interrupting. We'll get to that."

Hard as it was, I managed to keep my mouth shut. I'd keep my questions for when they were done talking. I had no doubt there would be more things to ask by then.

"After I turned your grandmother, I took her and your mother to your grandfather and told him the truth about what I was. What his wife had become. I gave Geoffrey a choice. He either helped me keep her turning a secret, or I told the council about her, and she disappeared from her family forever. To his credit, Geoffrey wouldn't give up on the woman he loved.

"He helped me keep her in the basement and feed her, until she tamed her hunger and could fend for herself. Then I helped her, your grandfather, and your mother relocate to London. We stayed in touch as they kept moving to a different city every five years or so, to avoid people asking questions. Your mother met Greg, who was visiting family in Cardiff, and soon she was pregnant with you."

"Greg and I got married first," Mom interjected.

"Yes, yes. Everything was done properly, of course. Anyway, once Geoffrey passed away, things changed."

"Oh God, please tell me you didn't sleep with my grandma."

He smirked. "I always loved my women feisty."

My horror must have shown on my expression, because Constantine laughed. "I never saw her that way, and I'm sure she never thought of me as anything other than a friend. What I was going to say was that, with Geoffrey gone, nothing kept your grandmother on that side of the Atlantic. When Kathleen decided to follow your father back to the States, your grandmother came too, and we decided to sever all ties between us."

"We trusted Constantine, but phone calls and letters leave a trail, and we didn't want to take any chances," my mom said. "Three months after you were born, we moved here and changed our family name."

"I didn't see either of them since and had no clue you were Kathleen's daughter when I met you. I'd still have no clue, if Ádísa hadn't made that comment about the women in your family," Constantine said. "It was then I started looking into things. Your grandma managed to steer clear of our vampire registry, since she wasn't turned in the States, and your parents stayed off the grid. It took a lot of digging before I found out you were Ross's granddaughter. Or, I should say, Ruby's granddaughter."

Ruby's granddaughter? "Aunt Ruby isn't your sister?" I asked Mom. My eyes felt about to pop out of my skull.

She shook her head.

Alex draped an arm around my shoulders and squeezed my arm. I more than appreciated his silent support.

"She's your mother?" I asked. "Ruby is Grandma Ross?"

Mom nodded. "She changed her name to Ruby after my father died. Said she wasn't the same person any longer."

"Well, fuck."

Dad laughed at mom's glare. "The girl got a shitload of family secrets shoved down her throat. Let her deal with it her own way."

I didn't see how he could make light of it. "Nobody thought to tell me all this before? I mean, *you knew vampires exist*. People in horror movies die all the time because they don't know the paranormal is out there, and you knew and didn't warn me?"

Dad's face fell. "We thought we were protecting you by keeping you away from that world."

Yeah, that hadn't backfired at all. I bit back the sarcastic retort when I saw the pain in his eyes. He and Mom did what they did out of love, and Constantine kept his mouth shut out of loyalty to them.

Their noble intentions didn't make me any less upset, but they did make me less verbal about my feelings. My head was spinning. This was all too much. Ádísa had attacked my grandma before having me turned. My former boyfriend was my grandmother's maker, as well as a family friend. I took a sip of the blood and made a face. It was cold and tasted of anticoagulant, yet I found it easier to swallow than what I'd just heard. I decided to take things one at a time.

"Aunt—*Grandma* Ruby visited in the middle of the day. How come she walked in the sun?"

Constantine's head snapped toward my mom. "She did what?"

Mom nodded again. "She has a secret brew that makes her tolerate sunlight. I keep a few bottles of it around, just in case. I've added it to your blood and Alex's tea, but it needs about three days of steady consumption to start working for more than a couple hours at a time."

Alex switched into detective mode before our very eyes. A determined look descended over his previously perplexed expression, and he let go of me so he could lean forward. "She has a secret brew? She came up with it herself? Is she a chemist or something?"

Mom shook her head. "Herbs. I've seen her mix them, but didn't recognize any, and she wouldn't share the recipe with anyone. Not even me."

That muscle on his jaw ticked. "And have you tested the limits of the brew? How long do the effects last at a time, once it kicks in?"

It was obvious he had more questions, but Mom held up a hand. "I don't know how she came about it, but she did. It was long after we moved to California. She returned from one of her trips in the middle of the day. Any testing that was to be done, she did herself.

"Anyway, she needed to stay below the radar, since your vampire council didn't know about her turning and she didn't know what they'd do to her if they found out. Trying to be prepared, she began keeping tabs on the council members. She keeps her vampire life away from the family, so she never let me in on how she does things, but she eventually managed to hack into the VSS archives and began recording new turnings."

This was incredible. "My grandma has solved the sun-allergy issue *and* is a hacker?" Ha. Coolest granny ever.

Constantine chuckled.

My mother cupped my chin, and the tenderness in that small gesture filled some hollow part in my chest. "She saw your birth name come up. Your father and I were devastated, but she convinced us it only meant we'd get you back eventually. When she tried to get more information on your whereabouts, she found the system had crashed."

"Yeah, the VSS was shut down soon after my turning," I said. It had been one of the consequences of my turning, actually. The old council, who'd established it, was overthrown by those protesting my semi-public turning. The new council members—including the two serial killers with world-domination aspirations, whom Constantine and I had dealt with—had decided to ban all new turnings. Without new fledglings, there was no use for the Vampire Social Services, the sole purpose of which had been to help newbies get used to their new life. "That's where I met Constantine. He was my sponsor."

"We had no idea. Your grandma never found out where you were. I've been waiting to hear from you since."

"Oh, Mom." I turned and buried my face in the crook of her neck, drinking in her familiar scent that I'd always associated with safety. When I raised my head again, I had to blink back tears. "I wish you hadn't killed Ádísa," I told Constantine, "so I could rip her head off myself."

He rubbed his temples, and I felt a pang of shame. Whatever else his maker had been, she'd been his near-constant companion for centuries, and he'd killed her for me. I owed him not to discount that sacrifice.

"So first grandma gets turned, and then I do. What are the odds?"

My mom let out a forced little laugh. "It's not just you two. I'm the only lucky one, I guess."

"Why do you say that?" Constantine asked before I could.

"My own grandma disappeared before I was born, but there were rumors she'd been slaughtered by a beast," my mother said.

Huh. The women in my family seemed prone to brutal attacks. When Constantine had proven his loyalty to me, not her, Ádísa had asked what it was about women in my family. My gaze locked with Constantine's. There had to be something there. But what?

Mom yawned, and I realized it was way too late for the humans among us. I sighed. Delving further into my family's past would have to wait one more day. My life was shaken enough as it was. Maybe I could spend the downtime raging at Constantine for keeping all this from me. His promise had been necessary to keep my parents safe, but I was no threat to them. He should have told me. And I really needed to yell at someone.

"Look at the time," I said. "We better get going. The hotel Constantine booked is close by, so we can be back here right after sunset. We'll pick things up then."

"Nonsense." Dad stood and pushed his chair back. "You're staying here."

"Dad, there's no room for us."

"Actually, there's a bedroom and extra pullout sofa in the basement," Mom said. "And we've installed a small bathroom. It's a little cramped, but you should manage for a few days."

The choice seemed as out of my hands as my unlife apparently was. I gulped down the rest of my blood, trying not to taste it, stood, and left my mug in the sink. "Well then, I guess we're staying. We just have to get some stuff from the car."

"Alex and I can fetch that," Constantine said.

"I'll help the boys. You ladies go make the beds." Dad kissed me on the forehead. "Goodnight, Princess. I'm so happy to have you back." He was so adorable, I didn't tell him *the boys* would probably need no help carrying the entire car.

"'Night, Dad. It's good to be back."

Mom wrapped one arm around my shoulders and led me down the hall. "You know," she said, tugging on a strand of my hair, "red really is your color."

It really was good to be back.

I'd been shocked and disconcerted—and was still more than a little pissed off at everything the people in my life had been keeping from me, but I was ultimately happy to be home.

Mom kept the subject light while we made the double bed. She told me Dad made her a small vegetable garden in the back yard, and how she'd love to have a cherry tree, but the climate wasn't right. I let the sound of her voice caress my ears. It had been forever since we last chatted about little, everyday things. It was so comfortable and soothing.

"Are you taking the sofa, or are you and Alex sharing the bed?" she asked, when we moved to the pullout.

There went the easy chitchat. "We live together," I blurted, smoothing an invisible crease on the bottom sheet. "All of us. Well, not *that* way. I mean, Alex and I live together *that* way, and there's also Constantine and three young vampires. And my friend Sheena."

"Is that all?" Mom was completely expressionless as she tucked in the corners.

"And Wesley. That's all."

She sat on the bed and pulled one corner of the light summer blanket on her lap. "Is it... Is it an actual relationship? Constantine has explained about vampires and polyamory."

"What? Oh, God, no. *No.* It's Constantine's place, and Wesley is his butler." I went on to explain the circumstances that lead to us all sharing a roof, and soon I was telling her about Alex's insistence we meet each other's parents.

"Oh, he introduced you to his mother? Things are serious, huh?"

I resisted the urge to say 'deadly.' "Pretty much, yeah. I don't know if he and I have the same ideas about the future, but we're as in love as can be."

Mom smiled and let out a rushed breath in what could only be relief. "So you're happy."

I sidled up next to her, so I could feel her warmth. "I am, Mom. And I'm so happy to see you and Dad again."

She placed a butterfly kiss on my temple, and I felt her smile.

Chuckles from the upper floor reached my ears. "The boys are back. You should go to bed."

She nodded and squeezed me, before getting up. "See you tomorrow, Gerri."

I didn't correct her. She needed to know some things hadn't changed, and if calling me by my old name helped, I'd play along.

****

"I swear to you, the only reason I didn't tell you was my promise," Constantine said when the humans of the house went to bed. "You have to believe me, but I understand if you don't. I've betrayed your trust before." His kicked-puppy look was as effective as Alex's.

My anger deflated. There was no use yelling at someone who didn't fight back, so I chose my next words carefully. "I get why you did it, but I still don't like it. I'm asking you one last time—is there something else you're keeping from me?"

"Yes." He didn't hesitate.

"Are you fucking serious?" Alex took a step toward Constantine, but I stopped him with a hand on his stomach.

"I want to know what it is," I said.

Constantine nodded. "Give me twenty-four hours to check the validity of my information, and I'll tell you."

"Twenty-four hours," I said. "And you never keep things from me again." I wanted to add 'or else,' but had nothing to threaten him with. I had to trust he didn't want to disappoint me again.

I had to trust a lot of things those days.

Constantine bid us goodnight and said he'd call home and let everyone know we were all right.

Alex got frisky as soon as the bedroom door was closed behind him. I didn't share his enthusiasm. Not with everything we'd found out.

Not with Constantine *not* sleeping right outside.

"My parents," I whispered. "They'll hear."

"I'll be quiet as a mouse." There was that smirk again—the one I didn't like. I'd never seen it on human Alex's lips. Constantine assured me we didn't lose our soul when we turned. I certainly felt the same person—if a little more street smart—but that nasty curving of Alex's lips made me wonder if that rule was universal.

Well, hello, paranoia. Constantine and my parents had hidden things from me, and now I was suspicious of everyone.

"I still feel weird," I told Alex. "I haven't set foot in this house in years, and I get laid the first time I visit?"

"That's not what bothers you." He undid my buttons so fast, I didn't realize my shirt was open until he peeled it off me. "You don't want *him* to hear."

I was too emotionally drained to get into a fight about his stupid jealousy. I framed his face with both palms and slanted my lips over his. "I don't want *anyone* to hear. I don't want an audience when we make love."

He undid my jeans and shoved them down with his knee. "You didn't mind an audience when you were in porn."

"And we're done here." I pushed him back hard enough to make him stumble and pulled my jeans back up. I told him about my past from the beginning, and he accepted it. I gave nobody the right to judge me for my choices, much less someone who claimed to love me. "You and Constantine can share the bed. I'm taking the sofa." I was so furious, I'd have sent him packing right there and then, if I didn't believe he was dealing with some sort of identity crisis.

Still, that excuse was wearing thin.

He got in my way, puppy eyes at full force. "I'm sorry, baby. I didn't mean it. It was supposed to be nasty-sex-talk. I guess I went overboard."

"You did."

"Forgive me? You know I love you."

"I know." But I wondered what his definition of love was these days.

He pulled me against his chest and kissed me gently on the lips. "We both know I've got the foot-in-mouth syndrome. Apparently dying doesn't cure that." He laughed, but I wasn't amused.

"Listen, Alex, I'm tired. I need to rest, and I need to figure out how to deal with everything. I'm really not in the mood."

He ran a hand down my spine and cupped my ass, oblivious to how genuinely angry I was. "I could try to get you in the mood."

"No."

"Sure?"

"Positive."

"Damn."

"Yup."

"Can we at least cuddle? And maybe I could have some blood?"

I couldn't say *no* to that. I burrowed in his arms and let him feed from my neck, until exhaustion got the better of me. "I need to be horizontal ASAP," I mumbled.

Alex tenderly licked his mark, then lifted me and carried me to bed. He dug in our overnight bag for my t-shirt and pair of shorts that acted as pajamas, and helped me into them. "Sleep tight," he said, spooning me from behind. "I'm here. Won't let anyone hurt you."

It sounded like an odd thing to say, since we were no longer on the run, but I was too tired to give it much thought.

Chapter Nine

Not used to keeping a human time schedule, I lay in bed for hours, staring at the wall and wondering if anything in my unlife was what I believed it to be.

I'd suspected before that Ádísa had issues with my family, but my grandma and me sharing the same fate had to be significant.

I already knew my turning hadn't been at random. A couple months ago, Constantine had confessed Ádísa had instrumented my turning and arranged for him to become my mentor. She ordered him to make me fall in love with him, and he was very successful in his mission.

Although he also fell for me and claimed he still loved me, she managed to seduce him while he and I were still together. I broke things off, and Constantine tried to get me back for years, before Ádísa's promises of power made him return to her side. That was when he found out about her role in my turning.

In the end, he chose me.

I remembered Ádísa threatening him with a sharpened stake for helping me.

"What is it with the women in your family, Cherry? No matter. Your allure worked against you this time. It got you where I wanted you. It's such a pity Constantine will share your fate, but maybe I'll get to keep your new friend."

She'd meant Alex, and I had no doubt she'd have gone for him too, if Constantine hadn't rid the world of her vile presence.

Alex tossed and turned beside me. Nightmares again. I couldn't blame him. Just weeks ago he was viciously attacked and left for dead. I thought I lost him, despite giving him my own blood.

Until Constantine brought him back to me.

"I really did and do love you, Cherry. I'd do anything for you, including sit back and let you be happy with a human." At the time, Constantine was playing the long game; Alex's life was finite, while my ex and I were immortal.

But Alex wasn't human any more, and Constantine was still letting me be happy with him.

Thinking of it was more taxing than thinking of Ádísa, so I steered my thoughts back to her. Assuming the rumors about her having been a Valkyrie—or as old as one—held merit, Ádísa was already ancient by the time my great grandmother was attacked. Too old to obsess about a woman she met a hundred-odd years ago.

Maybe I should look into our family tree. Go back further.

My vampire inner clock screamed that the sun was up, but I couldn't wait until the evening. Waiting is the thing I do worse. I even iron better than I wait. I sneaked out of bed, wrapped a blanket over my shoulders, and flew upstairs. Dad was gone for the day, but Mom was up and about, and she hurried to shut the drapes as soon as she saw me.

"Gerri, you shouldn't be up. The potion hasn't started working yet."

"I couldn't sleep. And please call me Cherry, Mom. I'm not the girl I used to be." My voice broke, and her hand trembled as she adjusted the blanket so it covered my head too.

"Big bad vampire or not, you'll always be my baby girl."

I could spare a few moments to be just that, so I burrowed into her embrace and stood there, listening to her heart beat. I hadn't realized how much I'd missed this. It had to be one of the reasons the council forbade fledglings contact with family members. Seeing my mom, having her hold me, reminded me of all I'd lost. Because of Ádísa.

She was no longer around, so I was going to find Willoughby and turn him to dust for the life he'd taken away from me.

I don't know how long Mom and I held each other, but when we let go, I felt an inner peace I hadn't experienced in a while. "I need your help," I said. "I need to figure out how far back Ádísa's thing for our family goes. What caused it."

"Hell hath no fury like a woman scorned," my mother said.

"All this, because Grandpa didn't choose her? If she was the one who attacked your grandmother, there had to be something before that. Do we have any old family photos? Notepads? Anything you can dig up? Maybe we could ask au—Ruby?" I couldn't really call her Grandma.

"She's in Europe for the next few months. She calls me every few days, but I can't reach her in the meantime. There are some boxes in the attic I've never gone over, though. I think I remember her lugging them around every place we've been."

"The attic it is, then."

She shook her head. "No curtains up there. You better stay here, while I go get the boxes."

I raised the edges of the blanket, forming batwings. "Nah, I'll brave it."

Mom smirked. "I haven't dusted in a while. There could be cobwebs."

Scary-ass vampire or not, I won't approach a spider, if I can avoid it. "I'll wait right here. You take your time."

She laughed and pinched my cheek. "I see immortality hasn't changed *some* things."

"Nope, spiders are still on the top of my phobias list."

"Good thing you have a good man to squash them for you now." Mom winked.

"Yeah, I'm lucky." I smiled, but my eyes stung.

"Uh-oh. What's wrong, honey? You seemed fine last night."

Mom could always see right through me. Even over the phone, she could tell when something bothered me, which was why I'd only been calling her sparingly once I'd decided to get into adult movies. I hadn't known what to say if she asked me about my career, just like I now didn't know what to tell her about Alex and me. Only this time, I wasn't afraid she'd disapprove of my choices. My fears and worries were too vague to be put into words.

"Nothing," I said. "This whole Ádísa mystery is stressing me out. Can you please get the boxes now?"

"Of course. I'll be right back." She kept stealing worried glances at me on her way up.

****

The boxes weren't a couple. They were eight, and one of them was as tall as me.

Mom got hold of an old hooded robe, and we replaced my blanket with it for ease of movement, before I followed her back to the attic. The robe was thick, but made no difference to me temperature wise, since vampires emanate no body heat. I pulled the hood up, kept my head down, and followed my mother's feet around the cluttered space, praying there'd be no spiders. With the two of us working together, it still took several trips up and down the stairs.

We began going through the boxes one by one, but their contents were in no order we could discern. In the end, I emptied them around us in messy piles. I could see the annoyance in my mom's gaze. She said nothing, but I knew her inner neat freak was having a stroke.

"I promise to put everything back myself," I said. "And I'll vacuum."

"Good." She heaved a sigh. "Now let's see what we have here."

For three long hours, we waded through old, faded pictures and frayed documents. Of the ones with dates scrolled on them, the oldest seemed to have been written sometime in the 1440's. The month and last digit in the year were nothing more than smudges on the fragile parchment, but I had no idea what was written on the legible parts of the note either. "I think it's in Italian."

"We can have Constantine translate it." Mom plucked it gently from my fingers. "Seems to be a letter to a Francesca."

"Was she our ancestor?"

She shrugged. "I don't know. Doubt Ruby would either, this far back, but I'll ask when she calls."

It made no difference either way. I found more notes and letters in the same writing and stacked them neatly one on top of the other, without bothering to look at them twice. As I lifted the tenth one in a row from the mess around us, a separate piece of paper fell from inside it. As large as my open palm, it landed face down by my foot.

Milano, 1447, it read on the back. I flicked it over and saw a drawing of a woman. It was a portrait, and not a very detailed one. The hair was pulled back, and she showed too little cleavage for what I'd known of Ádísa, but it could totally be her. I searched the drawing for a signature or name. Nothing but the place and date.

"I'll get Constantine. He might know where she was around that time," I said, shedding the robe. The sun was low enough by then that I no longer needed the extra cover, and the basement had no windows anyway. On the way down, I thought of waking Alex too, but maybe some rest would make him less confrontational.

At the entrance to the basement, I froze. Constantine was sprawled on the pullout, an arm over his eyes. The sheets only covered the bottom half of his body, and the part that was visible was naked. And smooth. And pale. And perfect.

Admiring beauty wasn't cheating, I told myself, but I still didn't let myself gorge on the sculpted abs and pecs, or the broad shoulders. What I focused on was his face. I hadn't seen him so serene in years.

Then again, I hadn't watched him sleep in years, though it hadn't been all that long since I'd last seen him naked.

"Constantine," I whispered, "we found something you need to see." No response. "Constantine?" I leaned in and lightly touched his arm.

Eyes still closed, he flipped onto his stomach, driving the covers lower and exposing the top half of an exquisite—and very naked—ass. I trained my gaze to the ceiling. I hated his habit of sleeping naked. Couldn't he have worn underwear for once? I considered going back up and having my mom fetch him, but that'd be an entirely new level of awkward.

"Is there some specific reason you're here at this ungodly hour, or are you just admiring the view?" His voice was muffled by the pillow.

I didn't take the bait. "You really need to get up. Have to show you something we found."

"Go away."

"No, seriously. You have to come with me."

"If I get out of bed with you here, I'll get accused of indecent exposure. What's more, I'm quite certain your boyfriend won't appreciate my reminding you what you've been missing."

I could say Alex's cock was just as big as his, or I could be a grown up. And damn it, it was a hard decision. "We found a drawing that might be of Ádísa. Do you know where she spent the 1440s? And wasn't there a war in Milan around that time? I think I remember something from The Borgias, but I was never good with dates." Naked asses make me ramble. Deal with it.

"What are you on about?"

He began to roll over, but I turned around before I saw more than a girl in a monogamous relationship should see of her ex. It didn't help much. I still recalled every detail of his naked body from his last attempt to seduce me, right after Alex and I got together. It didn't work then, and it wouldn't work now.

"Mom and I have been going over old family stuff. We found a drawing of a blonde woman, along with some letters. They're in Italian, but I looked for her name. She wasn't mentioned anywhere."

"That's because she was going by Adalgisa back then. I think I remember her being in Italy for part of the 15th century, but not exactly where. It's not as if we could Skype back then."

A rustling came from behind me, then springs creaking, and finally the sound of a zipper.

"You decent?" I asked.

Constantine heaved a sigh. "Constantly. Whether I want to or not."

That was true. He'd been way more decent than I'd had the right to expect him to be. He'd opened his mansion to Alex and me, never made a pass at me, and now joined us in this family-reunion-turned-quest-for-answers-to-an-age-old-mystery.

"You know, you're a good guy, deep down," I said and led the way up.

"It's a burden I carry with style."

Chapter Ten

I watched Constantine's face for a reaction, when my mother showed him the picture we'd dug up. All I saw was curiosity, while he perused every line. In the end, he agreed the woman on the picture could be Ádísa and spent the next hour and a half poring over the letters we'd decided were from that time.

"Nothing." He set yet another letter aside and readjusted his long, blond ponytail. "These are all from a gentleman named Mario to his young wife, Francesca, telling her how hard being apart from her is and how he longs to hold his daughter in his arms for the first time. I expect his wife is an ancestor of yours?"

"Your guess is as good as mine," Mom said.

I pursed my lips. "Probably, for the letters to have ended up here. You didn't find anything weird in them,

Constantine? Anything about a seductress trying to have her wicked way with him?"

"Nothing of the sort. I'm sorry." He looked sorry. Sorry and sleepy. "Wait. This is in different handwriting." He tilted his head to the right, narrowed his eyes, and leaned in to snatch the corner of a letter, barely visible beneath a pile of similar pieces of paper.

I should have noticed. Mom and I watched, as Constantine's expression grew cloudier with every line he read.

"It is from Francesca's mother, telling Mario her daughter was found dead. Savaged by what they believed to be a large animal."

"Ádísa. Has to be her. This goes too far back. Do we have a family name? Something that could help us figure out if Francesca belonged to a branch of our family?"

Constantine shook his head. "She only signs as, *Your Bereaved Mother in Law*."

So we knew Ádísa might or might not have been responsible for the death of a woman who might or might not have been our ancestor, six hundred or so years ago.

Which amounted to zilch.

"I got you out of bed for nothing, huh?" I asked Constantine.

"It appears so." He scowled. "But I may actually be able to help after all. Kathleen, is there a computer I can use? One with an internet connection?" I raised an eyebrow, and he chuckled. "Being a council member comes with certain…perks."

My mom led us to Dad's study room and logged on the computer. The perk Constantine had in mind turned out to be the council's database, complete with detailed profiles on all USA-registered vampires. Finding Ádísa's file wasn't hard, but the first entry on it was in the 1700s, when the first vampire governing body was put together and began issuing laws.

"Shit," I said, perching on the edge of the desk. "Is *nothing* easy with this woman?"

"Some things used to be." Constantine smirked.

I made a gagging sound.

"There's only more thing we could try, although I'm not sure what you're after," he said. "Assuming it was her, what good will knowing for sure do?"

"Try it. I want to find out how far back her grudge goes," I said.

"Went," he said.

"Huh?"

"How far it *went*. She's gone now, Cherry. Maybe you should forget about her and focus on spending time with your family. Soon you'll be able to go out during the day. Think of that and stop wasting energy on someone who's no more than dust."

"You're right, but I can't. I won't relax until I know why she hated us so much. Besides, Willoughby is still out there. How do you know they don't have the same agenda?"

"Willoughby?" Mom asked.

"My maker," I said. "He's Ádísa's childe and helped her with—with everything."

"About that…" Constantine's face darkened. "I told you there was a sighting. Go get Alex. He should hear this too."

"He should hear what?" Alex's voice came from behind me, and I snapped my head up. I hadn't realized how close to Constantine I'd drifted, until I saw Alex's gaze go from one of us to the other.

"I was waiting for confirmation, so as not to unnecessarily upset you, but it's official. Willoughby has been spotted in the area. Just two blocks from here, in fact," Constantine said flatly.

"What the fu—" I cut my question short at Mom's glare. "What the hell, Constantine? He might have come after my folks. Why didn't you say something sooner?" He and Alex were set on testing my limits. Couldn't a day pass without one of them driving me nuts? "You didn't think I might need to know that?"

"You had enough on your mind. I did not want to add to it."

I pretended not to notice Alex's smile. It wasn't as important as the realization I'd been making the same mistake over and over, allowing the two of them to think I needed someone to protect me. I couldn't blame Constantine for not knowing better. When we got together, I was a fledgling who depended on him for everything.

It was up to me to make sure he understood things had changed.

"New rule," I said, locking my gaze to his. "Now on, nobody makes my choices for me. You don't decide if I need to know something. If it concerns me even remotely, you tell me and let me deal with it. Is that clear?"

"I'm not reckless." Constantine scoffed. "I had people watching, ready to interfere and let me know if he reappeared."

I kept staring at him.

"Cherry—" He sighed. "We're clear."

Alex was still smirking, when I turned to him. "That goes for you too."

He nodded.

"Constantine, you said you had people. Who? We have vampire spies near my parents' house?"

"And humans," he said.

"Can they be trusted?" Alex came up next to me and draped an arm casually around my shoulders.

"Yes."

"Why are humans aware of our existence? Why do we have the whole stupid rule saying our families shouldn't know vampires exist, if there are other humans who do?" I asked.

"They're bite junkies." Constantine saw my questioning look and elaborated. "A sort of adrenaline junky, only with a more specific hit. They love the danger of having a vampire at their neck, as much as the euphoria brought about by controlled blood loss. They're usually among society's castoffs, willing to do anything for a fix."

"And you trust them?" I couldn't believe my ears. "Addicts aren't the most reliable sources."

"That's why the council doesn't take action against their existence. Because they lack credibility, they do not really pose a threat to us."

"And where do they say Willoughby is now?" Mom asked.

Constantine shrugged. "I have all my contacts in the area looking for him. He won't stay hidden for long."

"But the fact that he's here could mean Ádísa's issues with my family aren't in the past. Not really," I said.

Constantine huffed. "Let me pursue that alternate avenue I mentioned earlier."

So pretentious. I rolled my eyes, but didn't comment. Whatever his methods, he usually yielded results.

And he was hot—which didn't matter, because Alex was hot too, and I loved Alex. Solely.

Constantine left the room, thumbing the screen of his phone. I was tempted to eavesdrop, but held back. Now he knew I didn't need a protective bubble around me, I trusted him to come clean about whatever his call entailed.

Eerie silence, thick and heavy, filled the living room. Alex watched me quietly, which made me fidget. I fidget when I'm nervous, and his gaze unnerved me although I'd done nothing wrong.

"Sleep well?" I finally asked.

"Not enough." He looked around. "Must be the new surroundings."

Mom looked from one of us to the other. "Tea?" she finally asked Alex. "Or are you going back to bed?"

He beamed his most adorable smile her way. "I'd love a cup, thank you. Don't think I can sleep again. I'll come help you, and you can tell me embarrassing stories about Cherry's childhood."

Sneaky was the word that came to mind. I didn't like thinking that about Alex. He was simply being nice to my mom and seizing the opportunity to get to know her and me better. I'd have done the same in his shoes. It didn't mean he wanted to pick her brain without me hearing.

Constantine reappeared, a deep vertical line furrowing his brow. He seemed more contemplative than upset, as he tapped his phone against his palm, then slipped it in his back pocket. "That was Hui Zhong," he said. Hui Zhong was one of the two scariest council members. She'd been turned near the end of the 1800's and had gone on a spectacular killing spree before getting a grip on her hunger. You wouldn't know it to look at her China-doll appearance, but she was rumored to have been deadlier than the plague, back in the day.

"She said she knew nothing more about Ádísa than we do, but she'll ask Gheorghios and call me back."

I resisted the urge to make a face. As scary as Hui Zhong was, Gheorghios was worse. Vicious and quick to anger, he always seemed to me like the kind of man to slaughter first, ask questions later. Then again, appearances can be deceiving.

The council member I'd trusted most, Johnny boy, had been Ádísa's cohort, while Benjamin, who'd always made me uncomfortable, had turned out to be nothing more than a grief-stricken father looking for his daughter's killer.

They were both dust now, with Benjamin's position in the council taken over by someone I'd never met, and Johnny-Boy's by Constantine. Ádísa's spot was still open, and I prayed it'd get occupied by a peace-loving, knitting old lady who preferred watching cat videos on Facebook to plotting world domination.

"What exactly are you looking for?" Alex asked.

"More on Ádísa's past," Constantine said. "Anything to indicate what brought about her resentment for this family and whether Willoughby is planning to continue pursuing whatever nefarious plans she had."

"Sounds solid." Alex nodded. "Kathleen and I are making tea. Want anything?"

"I wouldn't mind some blood, if it's not too much trouble."

"None at all."

And there we were in Lala-land again, with the boys playing nice and creeping me out.

"I'm going to take the boxes back upstairs," I said. I used full vampire speed to stuff the contents back inside, then took my time carrying them to the attic.

Dad got home, and we all did our best to have a normal dinner, with Mom being extra chirpy and bubbly as she filled him in on the night's events. She'd cooked her signature pot roast with baby potatoes and accompanied those with a salad I didn't even glance at.

"Lucky we don't have to breathe between bites." Alex chuckled, and I realized I was wolfing my food like I'd starved for weeks.

"I've taught her not to play with her food." Mom batted his shoulder playfully. He answered with a boyish grin, and I liked that their short time together had brought them closer. It was important that my mom really like him.

I washed my bite down with some blood and daylight-serum combo. "I'm sorry, but this is so good. Better than I remember." It was the truth, but might be due to the enhancement of my senses more than to my mom's cooking skills—which were generally indisputable.

"It is delicious indeed. Kathleen, do I detect a hint of rosemary?" My ex, the foodie, ladies and gentlemen. I didn't listen to my mom's reply, too busy helping myself to a couple more slices of meat.

"Leave room for dessert," Dad said. I picked up chocolate chip cheesecake cupcakes on the way."

My favorite. I smiled. He smiled back. We all wore similar expressions of joy, as the conversation slid to a halt.

My expression was forced. I couldn't enjoy my lovely dinner, when there was so much we didn't know. So much we might have to deal with. I was convinced the lynchpin to the mystery was Ádísa's connection to my family. Once we figured that out, everything else would fall into place.

I sighed and decided to bite the bullet and ruin the faux-pleasant mood. "We should—"

Alex cut me off. "I don't want to be the party pooper, but I was thinking. About all of this." The shift in conversation seemed sudden, but the way he squeezed my knee said he understood I needed it.

To my mother, he said, "I know we're going by the theory that Ádísa was the monster who killed that lady in Italy as well as your grandmother, but why would she have spared you? If she had something against the women in your family, why not kill you too, when she attacked your mother? The connection is too flimsy. I'm afraid you could be seeing too much into things."

Constantine nodded. He swallowed his mouthful and wiped his lips with a napkin before he spoke. "That's a good point, Kathleen. Have you caught sight of her since she attacked your mother?"

"Ádísa would be hard to miss," I said, the roast going rubbery in my mouth. "With her height, long blond hair, usually mostly-exposed bouncy breasts, and her legs for miles—"

"You sure *you* didn't lust after her?" Constantine asked.

"I just got to take a good look at her," I whispered. "You know, when she was naked underneath you?" That shut him up.

"Thank you for the graphic description of her attributes"—Mom either didn't hear the last part of my comment or chose to ignore it—"but it wasn't necessary. I could never forget her. Haven't seen her since she turned Ruby, though."

That was weird. Not counting Francesca, who had lived and died centuries ago, Ádísa had apparently gone after my great grandma, my grandma, and then me. Did her attacks have some intricate pattern? Why would she have skipped one generation?

Alex held up his index finger. "I may be feeding into the paranoia here, but what about the men?"

"What about them?" I couldn't tell where his detective brain was going with that.

"Ádísa had issues with the women in your family, but what about the men? She was after your grandpa, right? Then she tried to get your ex. And succeeded." I didn't appreciate the reminder of Constantine's infidelity any more than I appreciated Alex's self-satisfied smirk. "Maybe she's after your men."

Our men—not only mine. "Dad, have *you* seen her?"

"I'd think I'd remember a tall, blonde warrior princess." Dad kept his gaze to his plate.

"Unless you weren't meant to," Constantine said.

I turned a questioning gaze to him.

He wiped the corners of his mouth with his napkin. "Humans can be mind-wiped."

Only not always perfectly so. Another vampire could bring the hidden memories back.

"Can you make him remember?" I asked.

Constantine nodded. "It's relatively simple. We can do it now."

Dad sat upright, fork still in hand. "Not sure I like the idea of you poking around in my head, trying to dig up memories that probably aren't even there."

Constantine's gaze softened. "Greg, you said you'd think you'd remember a tall, blonde warrior princess."

"Yeah, so?"

"Nobody said she was a warrior." Constantine arched a blond eyebrow.

My dad sucked in a breath, tension practically oozing from him. After a heartbeat, his shoulders sagged. "Do it. I'm ready. Whatever you need."

Before Constantine could work his mojo, Mom grasped my father's arm. "Tomorrow," she said. "I know we need to do this, but not now. We're having a nice family dinner, and Ádísa is dead. This can wait." I didn't blame her for stalling.

"No," Dad said. "We do this now. If this woman did something to me, I want to know."

Mom nodded in defeat, but Alex spoke up. "If you met Ádísa, whatever she made you forget wasn't pretty. Keep your blissful ignorance one last night. Enjoy the evening."

I squeezed his hand. "Alex is right. Eat up, I heard something about cupcakes. Then you go to bed, and we'll clean up in here. Maybe go for a walk after. It's a beautiful night."

Mom agreed with a sigh of relief, and she and my father soon left for bed. My parents still didn't have a dishwasher, but doing the dishes using vampire speed was a piece of cake for the three of us. Sadly, it lacked the sense of calm I used to get from menial labor in my human days.

"Let's go get that air," Alex said, as soon as the last glass was wiped dry and replaced in the cupboard. He tugged at my hand. "You coming, Cee?"

"I think I'd like to be alone for a while," Constantine said.

"See you later then. Call if you need anything; we'll be right outside." Alex went for the door, pulling me after him. I'd come to dinner barefoot, and didn't bother putting on my shoes as I followed him out the door.

Chapter Eleven

Outside, Alex asked, "You want to fly, don't you?"

I did. "How'd you know?"

"You're fidgeting. I know what you look like when you want space." He gave me a half-smile. "And you tend to take off, when normal people would take a stroll."

I ran a finger down his chest. "What about you? You hate flying."

He shrugged. "I don't have to come with, if you need to be by yourself. I can drive around, or do some after-dark hiking. Maybe visit the National Forest."

I loved him even more for being so understanding. "You sure you don't mind?"

His mouth found mine, and he nibbled on my bottom lip. "You need your alone time. I get it. Just be back by four, or I'll come after you." He narrowed his eyes in a mock-villainous scowl.

"Thank you." I kissed him again. "I love you."

"I know." He smacked my ass playfully. "Now go. Worry that pretty little head of yours till you're satisfied, then come back to me."

"Always." I let him walk to the entrance of the driveway, before I took off. I had no destination in mind. Just needed to feel the cool night air against my skin. And avoid dealing with my feelings.

At least I was practically a pro at the latter.

I ended up perched atop Agape Church. Agape means love in Greek, my father told me when I was a kid. For a long while, I'd thought I'd never have love in my life again. Now I did. I had Alex. I had my family back.

I had Constantine.

I should be feeling a lot happier than I was. Yes, horrible, unimaginable things could come up tomorrow, but my parents wouldn't allow the past to ruin their relationship. I shouldn't either. Only, I couldn't stop wondering why Ádísa had gone after my grandpa, possibly my father, and then Constantine.

I couldn't stop wondering how much of Constantine's betrayal—the betrayal that had broken us up more than four years ago—had really been his fault. And if it had been some kind of maker juju Ádísa had put on him, had he really been in love with me since we first got together? And was he still?

The past sucked. Most importantly though, it was over and done with.

I let myself slide down the shingled roof and fell to the ground, loving the rush of adrenaline despite the certainty I'd land on my feet.

The earth squelched under my bare toes, moist with the anticipation of rain. I decided to make a run for it.

I reached my parents' house well before four, but Alex was waiting for me outside. I jumped in his arms and bit the side of his neck. I grazed the skin, and the taste of his blood awoke a new hunger in me. I didn't want to feed; I needed to reestablish our link.

"I want you," I said.

"What about your parents?"

"We don't have to go inside. There's a shed in the back."

"And Constantine?"

Any answer I gave would be wrong. I closed my lips over his, to shut him up. I couldn't think about Constantine when I was about to make love to Alex. I dragged him to the shed and undid my jeans with one hand while pulling at his fly with the other.

"I need to be rough," he said.

"I want you to."

He bent me over a pile of logs and shoved my jeans down to my knees. A harsh tug, and my panties were gone. The night air caressed my pussy, and then Alex drove inside me all the way to the hilt. I dug my fingers in the wood. Splinters bit at my skin, and two of my nails broke, but I didn't loosen my grip. They'd grow back in the morning, and

I needed the pain. I relished it. Physical pain took my mind off my emotional turmoil.

Alex withdrew and plunged inside me again with enough force to make me lose my balance and scrape my legs against the logs. I could smell blood from the tiny cuts. It turned me on more. "Faster," I growled.

He found a punishing rhythm that soon had me crazy with lust. The first drops of rain pattered on the roof, the sound not loud enough to cover that of Alex's flesh slapping against the back of my thighs.

My pussy throbbed, my head felt light, and I was ready to fall off the edge, when Alex bit down on my shoulder, over my t-shirt. The bite was savage, tearing fabric and skin alike, but it was what I needed. With the first couple of pulls of my blood, he sent me spiraling toward my climax.

I was still floating, still fluttering around him, when he used his hands to rip the shirt open wider so he could lick the wound closed. "You're mine, Cherry. Say you're fucking mine."

The rain started in earnest, and the ground smelled of new life. One of my favorite smells. "I'm yours."

"*Not his.* You're mine." He swiveled his hips and began thrusting faster. Deeper.

I tried to adjust my position, uncomfortable now that the afterglow of my orgasm was fading. Alex grabbed my hair and pulled my head back, straining the muscles in my neck. "Not fucking his." He spat each word out.

I didn't need to ask who *he* was. "Yours."

He buried his fangs in my throat and sucked until my legs felt weak. Then he pulled out of me, and I felt his cum drench the tattered remains of my top and my exposed back.

My body was sated, but my mind was reeling. For all the niceties and buddy-routine, Alex felt threatened by Constantine, and his jealousy was affecting his behavior. That was what all the mood swings were about. Sheena had been right. He and Constantine were only civil to each other because they had to be. My parents' obviously liking my ex didn't help matters any.

Worse, I didn't know how to change that.

All I could do was keep showing Alex he was the only man in my life.

It'd be easier if that were the case.

Feeling dirty and guilt ridden, I let Alex help me to my feet and drape his own shirt over my shoulders. Arms around each other's waist, we walked back to the house and to the ground-floor bathroom, where we had a quick shower together. We tiptoed to the basement like naughty teenagers on a school night, making sure to remain completely quiet as we passed by where Constantine slept.

Safe within the confines of our bedroom, I trailed my fingers along the wound on my throat. It was already healing, but still throbbed. It felt out of place.

I didn't bother with pajamas, and neither did Alex. We lay back to back, but our feet touched. At some point, I heard Constantine say goodnight. I hadn't realized he'd been awake when we'd sneaked past him.

Alex didn't seem to hear, and I didn't answer. For all Constantine knew, I'd already gone to sleep.

Chapter Twelve

A knock on the door me woke me up, and I realized I was ravenous. I did a mental check of my state of dress and made sure Alex was covered.

"Come in," I said.

Constantine pushed in the room, holding a tray with baked goods and three steaming mugs. "It's ten past sunset," he said. "Kathleen brought us breakfast."

I nudged Alex, until he opened his eyes. "Food," I said and sat up, gesturing for Constantine to come closer.

He approached on Alex's side of the bed and handed him the tray, then lifted one of the mugs to his lips. "Whatever the secret ingredient is, it makes blood taste even crappier than the anti-coagulant does," he said. "How is it in tea?"

"It tastes a bit like sage. Or old oregano." Alex shrugged. "Not that great either way."

My mouth was already crammed with chocolate-filled pastry.

Constantine snatched a croissant. "Finish up and come find us in the living room. Your father is back. We're ready."

That almost made the chocolate goodness lose its yumminess. I had to take another bite to get it back.

"We'll be right up," Alex said.

We finished eating, emptied our cups, and got dressed.

Alex came up behind me and caressed my back. "It'll be all right," he said. "Whatever your dad remembers is in the past. She can't hurt any of us now."

I knew he was right, but I still dragged my bare feet to the comfy couch I'd spend a big part of my teenage years on. "Good morning," I said to my parents, though it was evening. I'd done that before too, after a late night out with my friends. I sat in the corner of the couch and pulled my feet under me. The comfy pillows hugged my body as if I'd never left, and for a moment it was as though the past six years of my life had never happened.

Only they had.

My father was in his favorite armchair. He looked a little pale, but smiled. "Let's see what I've forgotten," he said.

Mom stood next to him, holding his hand. "It'll be fine. Whatever it is, it'll be fine."

Constantine set one of the dining room chairs opposite my dad and took a seat. "Look into my eyes, Greg," he said. His voice had that deep, unearthly quality it got when he was enthralling someone.

Dad raised his gaze, and his face went slack.

"Greg, no matter what comes out of this, remember you are not to blame."

My mom bobbed her head in agreement. Having seen what Ádísa was capable of, I hoped she really believed it.

"You're not responsible for the things she made you do," Constantine said. "Will you remember that?"

"I'll remember," my dad replied in a flat, lifeless tone.

"Now focus on my voice. You and I are the only ones in the room. Nothing you say will hurt the people you love. Be completely honest. Have you met the woman we talked about yesterday? The tall blonde?"

"Ádísa."

"Yes. Do you remember meeting her?"

"I"—Dad's face distorted in agony—"don't know."

"She's told you to forget her. Forget everything that has to do with her, hasn't she?"

My father groaned.

"You're hurting him." My mother sounded scared. I jumped to my feet, but Alex stood and took her free hand before I could. I sat on the floor between them and Constantine, and smiled reassuringly at my dad. I wasn't sure he saw me, but I wanted to believe my proximity offered him and Mom some comfort.

"It's okay for you to remember," Constantine said. "You're allowed to. You're safe now. Tell me about meeting her."

"She said it's okay?" It was eerie hearing my dad sound so lost.

"She did. She said you can tell me everything."

Dad nodded. "Okay. I'll tell you everything. I met her when Gerri was eight. I had to stay late at work. On the way back, I saw a car stopped on the side of the road. A woman asked for help. It was her. Ádísa. I helped her change her tire."

"I remember that night," Mom said. "He came back covered in mud and said he'd slipped and fallen in the rain."

I remembered too. Mom had yelled at him for practically ruining his suit. The noise had jarred me from my sleep, and I'd padded to their room. My dad's face had broken into a huge smile when he'd seen me, and my mom had softened. They'd let me sleep between them that night.

"She was pretty," my dad said. "Beautiful. And she invited me to her hotel room. I said I was married. Had to get home to my wife. Ádísa got angry. Then she…" A tear sprung from his left eye, and I watched mesmerized as it coursed down his cheek to his chin.

"What did she do, Greg?" Constantine whispered.

"Maybe we should stop." I didn't want to hear more. Constantine should stop asking questions. He had to leave my dad alone.

"She looked into my eyes and told me she'd make me feel good. Better than my wife did. She bit me. It hurt, but she said I shouldn't fight, so I let her. She kissed me and pulled me down to the ground. She undid—"

"No need for details." Constantine sounded upset. I didn't know if he was jealous of Ádísa, or worried for my mom's sake. "Did you… Did you go all the way?"

"All the way."

Even though I'd been able to tell what his answer would be, my stomach lurched. Ádísa had mind-zapped my father into fucking her. Into cheating on my mother. I felt sick. This couldn't have happened.

Dad was all out crying now, the flow of tears at odds with his composed expression. "And then she told me to meet her again the next evening."

"I thought he was at work." Mom pulled free from Alex and covered her face with her palm. A surge of relief washed over me when I saw she hadn't let go of my dad's hand.

"Did you see her a lot after that?"

"Every evening for a month. After a while, she didn't have to tell me what to do. I'd hate myself and still do everything I knew she wanted. Then she'd tell me to forget until next time, and I'd go home. I'd leave the monster and go home to lie next to my wife."

"He had nightmares." Mom let out a sob. "He'd cry in his sleep. I should have known."

"You couldn't have," Alex said. It came out choked, but his tone was reassuring. "*He* didn't know. He probably felt something was wrong, or that something was missing.

Maybe he acted strangely, but his conscious mind had no idea of what was happening."

Constantine glanced at Alex, brow furrowed. I guess he didn't expect him to be so insightful. I knew better and was glad Alex was there for my mom when I was too crippled by shock and revulsion to be of any use. My heart ached for her, but more so for my dad. Recalling the memories was tearing him up inside.

"How did it end?" Constantine asked.

Dad smiled. "She asked if I loved her. If I would leave Kathleen for her. I was lucid enough to say hell no. What she'd made me do… I couldn't love a monster. Not when I had Kathleen."

"I'm amazed she let you live," Constantine said.

"She was furious. Said she'd drain me right there and then. I begged her to let me go. For my wife and daughter. Then suddenly she smiled. She said I could go and not come back. Said to forget her. That she could wait."

My head spun. My stomach roiled in disgust at what that woman had done to my family, and that didn't allow for the loathsomeness of her having slept with both my father and my ex.

I tried to refrain from lingering on that last part, as Dad went on. "I left. I forgot all about her. The nightmares stopped."

My mother shook her head. "Not completely."

"You'll have no nightmares of her again," Constantine said. "Ádísa raped you. You did nothing wrong. You'll remember it all, but it will no longer affect you. Now she's gone and can never hurt you or yours again. *Ever.* You're free from her. And now you're free from me."

My dad blinked rapidly and looked around, until his gaze focused on my mom. He pulled her in his lap, and they cried in each other's arms.

Constantine turned to me, and I saw the toll the whole thing took on him. His eyes were red rimmed, his lips tight. He stood, and before I could think about it, I leaped up and hugged him. "I'm sorry," he murmured against my hair. "I'm sorry I let her get to your family. To you."

"Not your fault," I whispered. My body was numb.

He withdrew, and Alex pulled me in a tight embrace. "Shhh," he said. "It's all behind you now."

I disentangled myself from him. "It's not only what she did to my dad. It's what she said when he turned her down. She said she could wait. Even when I was eight years old, she was planning on ruining my life. On having me turned. Why? Just out of spite?"

"I don't know." Constantine shrugged.

"Well, I'm planning on finding out," I said.

"We need to locate Willoughby." Alex traced circles on my shoulder with his thumb. "He's the only one who might know."

"We can get on it tonight. Now." Constantine seemed in a hurry to leave, but he didn't move.

I dropped to my knees in front of my parents. "Will you be okay?" I asked them.

My mother twirled a lock of my hair around one finger and gave me a warm smile. "We'll be great.

Constantine told us how he rid the world of that woman. She's gained nothing." Her eyes still shone with tears, and the neckline of her shirt was soaked, but she seemed to mean in.

"I love you." I smiled. My eyes burned, but I held the smile in place. We'd deal. All of us.

"We love you too, Princess." My father smiled too. "And we *will* be great. I feel lighter already. Thank you, Constantine."

"Think nothing of it." Unlike my dad, my ex seemed burdened with the weight of the world.

I wanted to hold him again, but it wouldn't go down well with Alex. "Thank you," I mouthed. I should say more, but the words weren't there.

I thought I heard him say he was sorry again, but his lips didn't move.

****

I watched Mom and Dad head upstairs. As soon as they were out of sight, I said, "We're going after Willoughby. Tonight. Constantine, any leads? Where do we start?"

"I suggest we start by scanning the neighborhood. If he is watching, we show him we are not sitting ducks. Odds are he will come to us. I do not believe he was sighted without his knowledge. Not when he managed to completely disappear for months. He wanted to lure us here." He could have shared that insight sooner. Along with other things.

Alex nodded. "I thought of that too."

"Either of you could have said something." My answer lacked bite. I was too mentally exhausted.

"It's just a theory," Alex said.

Constantine got the door. "Shall we?"

Within less than forty-eight hours, we'd found out that the ancient vampire who orchestrated my turning had been after our family for years, and she'd raped my father's body and mind. I felt drawn to Constantine on a level I couldn't explain; Alex had Mr. Hyde moments; and my aunt wasn't really my aunt, but my grandmother. Who was also a vampire.

Oh, and we were probably about to walk into a trap.

I needed a moment to process all that and analyze my dad's trip down locked-down-memory lane until it made sense to me. And I wanted a sounding board who had no horse in this race.

"You two go. I need to make a phone call," I said. "I'll catch up."

"Walking the streets alone two nights in a row is inviting trouble, especially if Willoughby's really still around. We'll wait for you outside." Or Constantine didn't want me to be alone after what we'd learned. I'd have expected Alex to be the one to object.

I nodded and waited for them to leave the house. Then I took a couple of unnecessary breaths and called Constantine's private landline.

Sheena picked up. "Have they killed each other yet?"

"No, but I'm tempted to off them both, for different reasons." I filled her in on what we'd found out and how much of it Constantine had known for a while.

Sheena snorted. "God. Men who pull that for-your-own-good crap drive me crazy. He's lucky he looks so good."

I laughed.

"And how's Alex? Going berserk, every time you and Constantine are within two feet from each other?"

"The paranoia factor keeps rising," I said, "but we're still holding strong."

"Promise you'll be careful," Sheena said.

"Don't worry about me. My guys have my back."

"Not the part of you they're interested in. You still promise."

"I promise."

"Good."

I hung up and returned to the living room. The sound of soft laughter drifted down from above, and I let myself hope things really would be fine. If my parents could share a laugh after the evening's revelations, anything was possible.

I pulled on my sneakers and stormed out. "Ready. Let's go." I slipped my hand in Alex's and silently prayed it wouldn't be long before this cloud pressing down on us dissipated. And what better way to speed that process than by finding and killing my maker? The grin on my lips felt slightly demented, but not forced.

Chapter Thirteen

Constantine, Alex, and I spent the next few hours patrolling the neighborhood, while pretending to enjoy a leisurely stroll. We meandered around my hometown in not-so-companionable silence, which I occasionally broke by pointing out a landmark or something I'd associated with my childhood.

"It's a beautiful place," Alex murmured, when we reached Santa Agape. "The whole town, I mean. A place to raise a family."

From the corner of my eye, I saw Constantine pick up his pace, allowing us some semblance of privacy.

"Alex," I said, "I'm sorry."

He gave me a questioning look. "For what?"

"You will never have the family you dreamed off." I had to be blunt. Our vague discussions about the future didn't seem to sink in, and after seeing my father cry for what was done to him, I was in no mood for subtlety.

"You don't know that." He shrugged. "There are other ways."

"No." I stepped up in front of him and held his gaze. "You can *never* have a family. You're no longer human. Children deserve to be kept away from our darkness."

"But with your grandmother's brew—"

"We'll still be vampires, even if we walk in the sun. The darkness is inside us. What will you tell your son or daughter, the first time they see your fangs pop out? They'll scrape a knee, have a nosebleed, and you'll vamp out instead of being there for them."

"Cherry—"

"*Never.*" I hated being that harsh and seeing the hurt and disappointment on his face, but there was no gentler way to break reality to him. I needed him to realize there was no maybe, no grey area, about this. "You're a vampire now. Not a human with a taste for blood. You don't get to live like them."

Constantine had tried to tell me that, repeatedly, and I'd shut him off, refusing to acknowledge the truth in his words. I'd been so wrong. On many things.

Alex nodded and kissed my temple. "You're right. I need more time to adjust to this change. Need to relearn how to think. How to be. You know?"

"I know." I found his lips with mine and kissed him gently.

"Maybe some tender loving can help speed up the process?" He nibbled on my lower lip.

"Not out here. When we go home. But you'll have to be quiet."

"Quiet as a vampire."

I laughed half-heartedly and swatted his ass. "Let's go. We have another ten blocks to cover."

I spotted Constantine by the creek. He was squatting next to a huddled figure. The wind blew the other way, and Constantine's face was averted, so I couldn't make out what he said, but the figure nodded. Constantine turned to us, and the moon shone on his face, revealing blood-smeared lips.

Alex tensed, flaring his nostrils. The human—had to be—stood and walked away.

Constantine used a handkerchief he pulled out of his pocket to wipe his mouth, and met us on the side of the road. "I promised him a bite for information," he said.

One of the bite junkies Constantine told us about.

"And? What did he say?" Alex sounded impatient, but I was sure the sight of blood had unsettled him. Feeding only from me was bound to become a problem sooner or later.

"He heard a girl was found nearby this morning. She was alive and lacking any physical signs of an assault, but appeared disoriented, and her blood-cell count was remarkably low."

"And he found all that out, how?" I narrowed my eyes. I didn't see the guy being into investigative journalism.

"His cousin is an EMT. He was first at the scene and followed the case."

"So we're sure her attacker was a vampire?" I asked.

"I'm certain it was Willoughby," Constantine replied.

"How?" Alex asked.

Constantine kept his gaze on me. "The girl was a redhead with bangs."

I took a moment to gather my thoughts. "That's not exactly proof." Even if it felt like a punch to the stomach.

"Forgive me, if I don't require more evidence. We obviously have to stay vigilant—maybe sleep in shifts once Ruby's potion takes hold, in case he has humans helping him."

Alex nodded. "Cee's right. We can't risk it."

I shrugged. There was no use disagreeing with the both of them, especially when I was still reeling at the thought of Willoughby attacking someone just because she had the same hair color as me.

"At least she's alive." Alex's voice was laced with relief.

"Maybe we should go by the hospital? See if she remembers anything?" I asked.

Alex shook his head. "I don't think it's a good idea. For all he knows, she's dead. If he's following us, and we lead her to him, he may decide to finish the job."

"She was really quite lucky. Willoughby isn't known to leave his victims breathing," Constantine said to him. His eyes were narrowed in speculation.

"Maybe she has a message for me?" I asked.

"As Alex said, we cannot risk leading Willoughby to her, if that's not the case. Let us wait until the potion takes effect. Then we can visit her during the day."

That made sense. We went on with our search, but found no sign of my maker in the surrounding area. I suggested we go looking downtown; San Luis Obispo has a rather lively nightlife, and nothing makes for better hunting grounds than nightclubs full of college students.

"He let the girl live. That has to be significant." Constantine tapped his chin with one finger. "He's not killing. He wants our attention, and he will have to stick close by to ensure his success."

I had to agree with that.

My thoughts veered back to the young redhead I'd never met. Whoever she was, she'd been incredibly lucky. Willoughby hadn't been all that gentle with me or with Alex; neither of us had survived his attack. His latest victim had been found in the daylight and had apparently been responsive, if disoriented, so she was still human. Still alive. If she was turned within three hours of sunrise, she'd remain dead until the next sunset, and if it happened earlier in the night, she'd be up and around by morning, but the sun would fry her.

Yup. Very lucky, indeed.

We were almost home, when Constantine's phone rang. Without breaking stride, he swept his forefinger across the screen and brought it to his ear. "Gheorghios, I did not expect you to call me back so soon."

I closed my hand into a fist with the thumb and pinkie extended, and shook it by my ear, waggling my eyebrows. The weird gesture was meant to ask for permission to listen in on the conversation. Constantine wouldn't be able to tell if I did, but I'd been brought up with manners.

He nodded, and I expanded my hearing.

Gheorghios was saying, "—if there's any truth in it."

"Tell me what you heard, and we'll look into it." Constantine came to a halt.

Alex and I stopped walking too, and I widened my eyes at Constantine. I wasn't sure letting Gheorghios know we were together was a good idea.

"We?" Gheorghios asked.

Constantine snorted. "You have been a council member longer than I, Gheorghios. You know we each have our people." Good save.

"Of course."

"So, if you please…?"

"Yes, yes. As I told you, all I know is a legend that some of the oldest among us believe to be about her. I cannot vouch for its validity. "

He paused, but Constantine remained silent.

"According to legend, Ádísa was a Valkyrie who fell for a mortal," Gheorghios said. "She was supposed to collect his soul, but the man promised her his love, and she let him live. Odin, the father of the Norse gods, made her human as punishment. She would only be allowed back in Valhalla, if she brought with her the man's soul, but he had to give it to her willingly. Ádísa said she did not care about immortality;

she would live out her human years with her lover. When she went to him, however, the man told her he was in love with another woman. He'd lied to Ádísa on the battlefield.

"Ádísa was enraged, but she no longer had the power to harvest his soul and take it to Odin. She begged Odin to take her back and reinstate her powers, and he said he would do so only if she managed to gain the man's love. Despite her pleas and promises, the man showed her nothing but scorn. He gloated over having fooled a Valkyrie.

"The thought of growing old and dying alone terrified Ádísa. Crazy with loss and sorrow, she found a vampire to turn her immortal again, and then killed the man who betrayed her. When she offered his still beating heart to Odin, the father of gods finally took pity on her. He said there was a way for her to return to his side. She had to win the heart and soul of a man pledged to a descendant of the woman the human chose over her."

I caught Constantine's gaze. He frowned. "So am I to believe in Old Norse mythology?" he asked Gheorghios. "I lived those times. I don't remember any Valkyries around for my death."

"Believe what you will. I only told you what I have heard. I know of no one who asked the lady herself and survived to share her answer."

"I see. Thank you, Gheorghios."

"Just remember your promise."

What promise?

"I do."

"When time comes, I shall call on you," Gheorghios said, and Constantine terminated the call.

"What promise?" Alex asked before I could.

"Nothing significant. Vampire politics." Constantine waved him off.

"You were a Viking," I said. That he was actually ancient never ceased to amaze me. "Ever hear of that legend before?"

"Not that I recall. What do you two make of it?"

I didn't know what to think. I wasn't sure what I'd heard. Was all this possible? "If we believe what Gheorghios said—and that's a big 'if'—I guess my great-great-great-several-times-back-grandma could have been the other woman. It would explain Ádísa's mania to destroy my family, and especially her hatred for me. I was turned before I had any kids, and she didn't know Ruby isn't dead, so I was her last chance. The last of our bloodline. She needed to seduce a man who loved me, to get her place back. But seriously, do we even believe this story? I mean… gods and Valkyries?"

Constantine's face fell. "Improbable though it seems, it would explain a lot."

I put two and two together. "Was this why Ádísa had me turned? Why she told you to make me fall in love with you?" It wasn't the most appropriate conversation to be had in front of Alex, but propriety wasn't my main concern right now.

"Possibly."

"She had to know you'd fall for Cherry too," Alex said. "It wouldn't have worked otherwise. She had to steal you from her."

She had stolen him, hadn't she? I'd found Constantine fucking her on the bed he shared with me. Her face shone with triumph, as she'd looked up at me. "She thought she'd won," I whispered.

But she hadn't. Because Constantine's heart had remained mine.

It still was, if I were to believe him, despite the three young vampires spicing up his nights lately.

I don't know if Alex caught the longing in Constantine's gaze. It only flickered there for a second, but that was enough for a knot to form in my stomach. Constantine and I had been Ádísa's puppets for years, our relationship constructed and shattered by her hand. I saw him clench both palms into fists and then relax them.

"Once again, glad you killed her, man." Alex patted Constantine's back. I couldn't tell if he was oblivious to my ex's discomfort, or was trying to alleviate the tension.

Constantine's reply was too low even for my vampire hearing to pick up. He didn't speak again till we were home. Neither did Alex and I. My parents were asleep, but there was a platter of sandwiches and three cupcakes waiting for us in the kitchen. We grabbed a bite and drunk our fill of Ruby's magic potion—Constantine and I with blood, Alex with more tea.

Alex tried to boost our spirits by suggesting daytime trips once the ability to walk in the sun kicked in. Where he found the strength to remain upbeat was beyond me, but it was equal parts endearing and annoying. I can't speak for Constantine, but my mood wasn't improved.

Chapter Fourteen

Sex was the furthest thing from my mind, when I finally stretched my body on the mattress. My lack of sleep caught up with me, and all I wanted was to close my eyes and wake up in a week.

I couldn't blame Alex for not sharing my vision. He was better rested than me. Better fed too, since I had packaged blood as sustenance, while he drank straight from the source—also known as me.

"Are you too tired?" he asked, raising the hem of my t-shirt and rubbing circles on my back.

"Mm-hmm, but what you're doing feels nice."

He kissed me behind the ear. "I can let you sleep, if you want."

My mind said, *yes, I'd truly appreciate that*, but my body already responded to his touch.

"I'm up for some gentle lovin'," I said, and smiled into my pillow when Alex blew cool air down my spine.

"What my lady wants, my lady gets." Slowly, almost lazily, he ghosted his fingertips down the length of my body, lighting my skin on fire with feather-light caresses. "I love touching you," he whispered in my ear, his breath warm with my blood.

I rolled on my side, facing away from him, and pushed my body into the curve of his. The planes of his chest and abs felt like living marble against my back, as he ran his open palm from my throat to my breasts, and then down my stomach. His fingers were rough, callused with years on the force, but his touch was as soft and tender as the kiss he laid on my shoulder.

I spread my thighs in invitation and draped a leg backward over his thigh, opening myself to his exploration. He briefly cupped my mound over my panties before he returned his attention to my breasts, slowly kneading each in turn.

"I want you," I said. "Gently, but now."

He chuckled in my hair. "You're the personification of patience."

I growled. "In me. Now."

He pulled my underwear to the side and slid inside me slowly, filling me up until his pelvis was flush with my ass. Then he began the exquisite torture of gliding in and out of me one inch at a time, stoking the fire inside. I rocked against him languidly, both turned on and lulled by the swaying rhythm of his strokes.

There was no moaning, no panting, just a steady, quiet climb to pleasure.

He slipped two fingers between my folds and circled my clit in tandem with his thrusts. I could stay like that forever—my body tingling with sensation, and Alex pumping slowly inside me.

My orgasm had a different idea. It sneaked up on me, and the waves rocking me suddenly sent me crashing over the edge, the assault on my pleasure sensors so immense, my vision blurred. My limbs went rigid with the effort to contain the feeling of utter bliss.

It couldn't be contained.

Among the craziness and chaos that was my life, this connection with Alex—this perfect synchronicity of our bodies—kept me in check. Because of him, I could be happy.

"I love you," I said.

He spilled inside me as, tears sprung from my eyes. This man was perfect for me, and I was so lucky to have found him at a time when everything around me was collapsing. So lucky his turning hadn't taken away everything that made me love him.

"I love you too," he said. "So very much."

I drifted off still linked to him. Still happy.

My dreams wouldn't let my happiness last. In them, Alex finished his declaration of love with another woman's name.

Ádísa.

I snapped awake, feeling an eerie cold. It was a weird sensation, to say the least; due to our low body temperature, vampires are way more sensitive to heat than cold.

"Alex?" I whispered.

Nothing.

I turned to look at him, but his side of the bed was empty.

"Alex?" I said again, as if calling his name could conjure him out of thin air. He was probably taking a shower. But I heard no sound of running water. Inexplicable dread dug talons in me.

I got out of bed and pulled on my jeans, not bothering to change my top or wear a bra. My cell phone lay on the floor by the bed. I picked it up and checked the time. Almost seven in the evening. The sun was low, but not down yet.

Careful not to make a sound and wake up Constantine, I left the room and climbed up the stairs. At the ground floor landing, I sucked in a useless breath. Now we'd see if Ruby's potion really worked.

Scrunching my nose in anticipation of scorching pain, I held my hand out to a patch of light.

Nothing.

A beam of bright afternoon sun sliced my palm in two. Painlessly. I turned my hand, fingers up, and waved it through the light. Gentle warmth caressed me. I didn't need more proof. Ruby had done the impossible; she'd given us back the day. Now I was going to make sure Alex didn't do anything that would stop him from sharing it with me.

I was out the door in no time, despite Mom's warnings that the potion's results were short term at first.

At the end of the driveway, I sniffed the air. Bad choice. I hadn't been out in daylight in a long while, and even the scent of freshly cut grass was different than it was at night. It was disorienting, until I decided to tone down my sense of smell and try another way. A quick glance around revealed no onlookers, but I'm not sure the existence of witnesses would have stopped me from taking off.

Maintaining a high enough altitude that I would look like a large bird to anyone happening to look upward, I scanned the surrounding area. There he was, entering the woods. I made as inconspicuous a landing as I could and hurried after him. It wasn't hard keeping track of him; he was walking at zombie pace and seemed more asleep than awake. I thought of calling out to him, but something held me back. I wanted to see how it all played out.

I waded through the trees after him, scrunching my nose every time I stepped on a dry twig or my movements sent a bird or little animal scurrying. I needn't have worried. Alex was oblivious to my following him. Gradually, my steps became bolder, until I was only a couple feet behind him by the time the trees began giving their place to tall shrubs.

We'd reached the edge of a small clearing, strewn with grass that seemed to have been stepped on once too often, the green blades no longer making an effort to stand. The place seemed as good a picnic spot as any, complete with a handful of logs that came up to my knee and could be used at seats. We were lucky there were no families around, in case the sleepwalking vampire in front of me woke up feeling grouchy. Alex sat on one of the logs, his moves deliberate. I rounded the clearing until I was almost facing him, trusting the foliage to conceal me.

Had he come here before? When? When I'd gone flying by myself? I'd have seen him. Before I could figure that out, he spoke. "Are you there?"

I thought he was talking to me and took a step forward, before I realized his eyes were closed. I'd been right. He was sleepwalking.

Someone apparently responded in his dream, because Alex smiled and turned his face upwards. "Don't worry," he said. "Nobody knows. It's our secret." He nodded.

He seemed so absorbed by whatever reply he got, for a moment I was convinced someone was speaking to him. I looked more intently, trying to make out a shape. Nothing. The forest had gone quiet around us too. I rubbed my arms. Despite the mild weather, I was chilled to the bone. And getting more creeped out by the minute.

Alex opened his eyes, and I thought he finally woke up, but his gaze was unfocused. "Cherry loves me." He said something else, but it was little more than a breath, and I didn't catch it.

I heard a hiss and looked around, but the sound had come from Alex. He was smoldering. Like, literally. The potion was apparently wearing off, and plumes of smoke wafted off him. No longer mindful to stay hidden, I ran to him, calling out his name. He sat there, smiling, so I threw him over my shoulder and flew us home as fast as I could, trying to keep his face shaded and praying nobody saw us.

When I returned Alex to safety, Constantine was up, prowling the limited space of the basement like a caged animal. "Is it true? Did you really walk in the sun?" He sounded like a little boy asking if Santa was coming. "I wanted to see for myself, but the older we are, the more brutal the sun."

I couldn't help a fleeting smile. "Yes. But it wore off fast, and Alex is burned."

Constantine was all-business in no time. "What do you need of me? Blood?" He reached for Alex's prone form.

I shook my head. "I've got this. I'll need to run something by you after I feed him, though, so maybe don't go too far."

"Or I could stay here and help you."

I wasn't very comfortable with him watching as Alex drank my blood, but I needed to pick his brain about the one-sided conversation I'd witnessed. I sat on the pullout Constantine used as a bed, and my ex helped me lay Alex down so I cradled his head on my lap. I popped a vein in my forearm with my fangs and held the wound against Alex's lips. He remained motionless, but I could see his throat working, so he was swallowing at least some of it.

"It will not be enough," Constantine said. "Our bodies do not work the same way human bodies do, and our circulation is much slower. He needs to suck to keep the blood flowing, or you'll heal before he feeds."

"He will. Give him a minute."

A couple of seconds passed, before Alex's mouth turned firm against my skin, and soon his fangs extended. In as much pain as he had to be, with patches of skin on his face and arms burned almost to a crisp, he was surprisingly gentle reopening the wounds I'd made, and sucking my blood.

"You are too calm for someone whose lover was minutes from turning into charcoal," Constantine said. His tone was glib, but his gaze searched my face.

"Once I got him inside the house, I knew he'd heal." I was right. Blackened ashy flakes peeled away, and tissue rejuvenated in front of my eyes.

"He was lucky you were there, although I cannot fathom why the two of you decided on a midday stroll all of a sudden." Constantine arched a mocking eyebrow, but dark violet swirled in his blue eyes. The way they changed color, betraying his emotions always mesmerized me. From past experience, I knew violet came with a primitive lust, completely inappropriate for our current situation.

Another thing for me to lock away deep inside and pretend not to have noticed.

I turned back to Alex's face and gently removed my wrist from his mouth. His face looked tired, but the flesh was now intact. Perfectly smooth.

"We didn't go for a walk," I told Constantine, gazing at him again. "Alex was sleepwalking, and I followed him."

"Sleepwalking?" Constantine's eyes were their normal clear blue now, his focus on the information I provided.

"Yes. It was weird. He was walking like he was a puppet on a string, but purposefully at the same time. More robot than zombie, if you know what I mean." Constantine nodded, and I went on. "He stopped in the middle of the forest, sat on a log, and began talking to someone I couldn't see." I shivered—which I rarely ever do since I died.

"That *is* weird, as you so eloquently put it. *Freaky*, even, as Sally would say. Did you make anything out? What did he say?"

"He said nobody knew… something. I don't know what he was talking about, but I think it was a secret. Could be about his turning?" And he'd said I loved him, but there was no reason to bring it up.

"Has he done this before? Does he have nightmares in general?"

"Yes to the nightmares, no to the sleepwalking. At least, I think it's a no. We'd have noticed if he'd walked out of the mansion in the middle of the day, right?"

"Maybe we should ask him?" Constantine indicated Alex with a tilt of his head, and I saw Alex's eyes were open.

"You're awake." I ran my fingers through his hair. "You scared me. I'll start locking the doors when we sleep."

"What? Why?"

"You up and left, with the sun still high in the sky." Constantine tutted.

"I did?"

"It was in your sleep. Do you remember what you were dreaming of?" I whispered.

He sat up abruptly. "No. You, I think. And Willoughby. It's all a blur."

"Do you remember the secret?" Constantine asked.

Alex's expression went from alert to slack and back again in the blink of an eye. "Secret? What are you talking about?"

I glared at Constantine. Alex was in shock; we shouldn't be grilling him until he got his bearings. "You mentioned a secret when you were mumbling," I told Alex. "It was probably nothing. Dreams don't always make sense." I leaned over and touched my lips to his.

"Yes. I remember now. It was… It was the vampire council, and they were asking who knew I was a vampire. I told them it was a secret and nobody knew. I was terrified."

No. He'd been smiling at the time. Conspiratorially. Had he lied to my face, or did he actually remember wrong? Something in my chest tightened, liquefying my insides. My gut was telling me not to trust him.

He took both my hands in his, and drew circles with his thumbs on my knuckles. His touch sent an unpleasant tingle spreading up my arms. "I'm sorry I worried you. I guess my subconscious made me want to distance myself from you, to protect you."

I don't need to breathe, but I felt suffocated by his proximity. I forced a smile. "All's well that ends well. And now we know Ruby's potion has started working, so that's something."

Also, I was now certain he was lying. Asking him about it wouldn't help, when the lie had spilled out so easily, so I had to watch him and pray he had good reason to keep the truth from me.

Alex grinned, our previous discussion already forgotten. "Does that mean we can have a picnic?"

"It still wears off too fast, but in a couple of days…"

"Good." He pulled me to him for a kiss that lasted a couple seconds more than was appropriate in front of company. By the time we parted, Constantine was no longer in the basement.

Chapter Fifteen

We were in the kitchen, having a civilized meal with my parents, and all I could think about was how Alex had lied. I couldn't fathom the reason. What could have been so bad about his dream that he was afraid to share it with me?

I tried to make sense of what I'd seen in the clearing, but something kept nudging at the back of my mind.

He'd been walking, not wandering. He'd meant to go to that specific spot. Sure, it was possible he remembered it from our search for Willoughby the night before. He was a cop, trained to be perceptive and remember details. But had one short jaunt through the woods been sufficient for him to memorize the path? Even the stupid log he'd sat on? He hadn't stumbled once.

I needed to look up how sleepwalking worked. Maybe he actually saw the scenery around him, and I was driving myself crazy for no reason.

"Want some more pasta salad?"

"Huh? Yeah, thanks." I lifted my plate for Alex to serve me two more heaps of the yummy combination of pasta, smocked tuna, corn, carrot, dill, and capers—with enough mayo to clog the arteries of the humans at the table.

He studied my face. "Are you all right? You haven't said a word since we sat down."

Dad piped up, always to the rescue even after all the years I wasn't around to be his little girl. "She's probably still excited about walking in the sun. It's been a while."

It really had, and I didn't even have time to enjoy its warm caress on my face. Not with Alex being a weird robot from planet Weirdo.

The thought I couldn't quite form glided just past the edge of my conscious mind. I tried to snatch it, but it swam away, fast as lightning. Stupid thought.

"Yeah, everything's been so overwhelming." I smiled at Alex and gave his hand a light squeeze, before turning my full attention to the food. "This is really good."

Mom beamed. "I knew you'd like it. And I have ice cream for after."

It was a lucky thing we couldn't gain weight after our death. Not so lucky that we couldn't lose any, but oh well.

"Are you going to look for that man again tonight?" Mom always had a way of making things sound normal. The homicidal vampire who'd turned me and left Alex for dead was now *that man*. Just like Ádísa was *that horrible woman*, and I was still alive.

Alex's fork hovered in front of his mouth for a second too long. He didn't like the idea. Maybe a confrontation with Willoughby scared him. Maybe that was what the dream and his irregular behavior had been about.

Sadly, I was sure he'd been enjoying himself at that clearing.

Worse, I was afraid whatever he kept from me was sinister. Something he wanted to keep to himself, not to protect me from.

My phone rang in my pocket. I was entirely too willing to let it go to voicemail, but it might be something important. I pulled it out. Constantine's home number.

"Everything okay?" It would be Sheena. I couldn't imagine Wesley or any of the vampettes calling me instead of Constantine.

"Here yes. There… not so sure." I could picture one perfectly shaped black eyebrow arched in reproach.

"We're managing." I pushed my chair back. "I'll be right back," I said to my table companions and went to the living room. The more distance between me and the other vampires, the better the chances they wouldn't listen in on my conversation. They both supposedly had better manners than that, but I wanted to keep my ass covered in any case.

"Alex is being weird," I whispered in the receiver, once I was reasonably sure of my privacy.

"Maybe he's sniffed out Willoughby," Sheena said. "Wesley told me to call you. He tried tall-blond-and gorgeous, but the call wouldn't go through. We got word your maker is there and planning something nasty." She pronounced the word as nay-stee, pouring gallons of distaste into it.

I knew she used theatrics to cover her fear of him. He'd threatened to kill her more than once, after all.

"Do we know specifics?" I asked. "Like maybe where he's staying?"

"Do you want his bank account number too? No, we don't know specifics. There have been sightings of a tall, dark, and handsome vampire terrorizing that area. Resident vampires have taken it upon themselves to clean after him, but nobody wants to go up against him."

One sentence had spawned a myriad questions. I decided to start with what I deemed as most important. "Terrorizing? There have been more attacks than the one we know of? Are the victims dead?"

"Don't know who you know of."

"A young redheaded woman."

Sheena blew out her breath noisily. "Hon, he's attacked three young women, and they're all redheads. Good news is they're alive, and the vampires of the area have made sure they don't remember their attacker."

So much for the red hair being a coincidence. It's impossible for us to get migraines, but I swore a spot behind my left eye throbbed. I pressed the heel of my hand against my temple, willing away the phantom pain. "Why?"

"Because there would be chaos, if the whole town knew undead monsters walked among them? Why do you think?"

I wanted to return her snappishness, but reminded myself it wasn't Sheena I wanted to kill. Slowly, as if talking to a child, I said, "No, I mean why does he leave them alive and not bother to alter their memories? That's not his usual MO."

"Maybe he wants to cause chaos? How should I know how a psycho vampire thinks? Just, please stay safe."

"I will." I was about to hang up the phone, when another question popped up. "Sheena, how do they know it's him?"

She snorted. "He's the only vampire unaccounted for in the census, and the description matches his."

"Is *tall, dark, and handsome* all they've got? What about his clothes? The color of his eyes, maybe?"

"I have to check up on that, but I think Wesley said he looks casual and inconspicuous. Nothing that sticks out too much. I'll get back to you on the clothes—and I doubt anyone got close enough to see his *eyes*, Cherry."

My fingers went numb, and I almost dropped the phone. Casual was not a word that would ever describe my maker. It did, however, fit another tall, dark, and handsome *unregistered* vampire. "No need." I tried to sound calm, but my voice shook. "Won't make a difference anyway. We know whom to look for."

But did we?

"Call me if there's any development," Sheena said. "And tell Constantine to check in more often. Mini-yous are having withdrawals, and it's like PMSing to the power of bitch."

I laughed, but my heart wasn't into it. "I'll tell him. Talk soon, babe."

"And call me if you manage that threesome."

This time my laugh was a little more real. I hung up and turned around.

Constantine leaned against the wall. Vampires can be stealthy, but it still amazed me how a man his size could move around so quietly. He was close enough to touch, and I bet he'd heard Sheena's naughty parting words.

Fuck.

Or not, if I didn't want Alex to kill us both.

The thought sobered me. Alex and killing was nothing to joke about. Not if my train of thought wasn't widely derailed.

"I need to talk to you," I said to Constantine in a hushed tone. "But not here."

"Are you going to try and lure me into the threesome your friend mentioned?" His voice was as quiet as mine. "You know I won't need much convincing, but I'm rather certain your boyfriend will be less open-minded."

So he wasn't going to let that drop. Eh, I was still free to bypass it. "Something is seriously wrong. Maybe we can find some way to sneak away for a few, later? I don't want Alex to hear."

He shrugged. "Then speak freely. His mother called, and he stepped outside to take it."

I inhaled deeply—I may not need air to survive, but I need it to speak, and I had to get the words out fast. Before love and loyalty stifled them and risked everything and everyone around me. "I think it's Alex. I think he's the one attacking women."

Constantine arched an eyebrow. "Your gallant knight? What makes you say that?"

"I don't have specific proof. Just a gut feeling. He's been acting weird. Hiding things, bringing up obstacles to finding Willoughby... Remember he was the first to say we shouldn't go see Willoughby's victim at the hospital? Maybe he was afraid she'd recognize him. And according to Sheena, Wesley spoke to someone who said Willoughby has attacked two more redheads in the area. Only he doesn't wipe their memories. The locals do."

And who were the local vampires in San Luis Obispo? How come I hadn't noticed any nocturnal neighbors when I still lived here?

Then again, I hadn't noticed my *grandmother* was a vampire—or that she was even my grandmother.

"Willoughby must have a reason for doing that. To create panic, possibly, or draw out the local undead population for whatever purpose. What does that have to do with Alex?"

"Your spies only think the vampire doing it is Willoughby because of his physical description and 'cause he's the only one whose whereabouts aren't recorded in the census."

"So…?"

"They said he's—as Sheena put it—*casual and inconspicuous*."

"That would be out of character for Willoughby. He is a pretentious prick, after all." The words were ironic, coming from someone who lived in a mansion, but at least Constantine deigned to wear jeans and a T most days.

"Also, kind of important, Alex isn't even *in* the census," I said, pulling my thoughts away from Constantine's stylistic choices.

Constantine pursed his lips. "What you're suggesting is highly improbable. We—You've been with the man near constantly."

"Except for when he sleepwalked. What if he's done it before?"

"He didn't back home. He'd have burned to a crisp. Even if he'd found a way around that before the potion, there are alarm systems in place at the mansion. He couldn't have wandered off."

"Plus we'd have heard about more attacks," I muttered. "It doesn't make sense. Why here? What triggered his sleepwalking?"

"It could still be a stand-alone event, Cherry." Constantine gave me a smile that would have been reassuring if I didn't know him enough to make out the doubt in his eyes. "He could have dreamed of something that made him walk to the woods."

I huffed and blew my bangs out of my face. "It's more than that. I know it. Something has gotten to him." Could be the same something that had toned down Constantine's sarcasm since we got to my home town. My family? The sense of belonging… or not?

"If that's the case, what has changed in his circumstances? Think, Cherry."

"If it's not late-onset fear of commitment, it could be Ruby's potion. He could be allergic, or something." Fuck, I really didn't want the potion to be at fault. I wanted us to keep taking it.

"I somehow doubt it's either." Constantine inched closer and traced his thumb along the wall, right by my shoulder. I sensed his need to touch me, but couldn't allow myself the comfort of his touch.

I took a step back. "Whatever it is, we have to watch him. Constantly. I think whatever he's dreaming of is making him dangerous. Maybe it's that he won't drink blood. Maybe his subconscious craves it, and he goes after humans in his sleep."

He dropped his hand and nodded.

"Honey?" Mom's voice came from the kitchen. "Will you get the boys and come back to the table? It's dessert time."

"Sure, Mom," I called back. To Constantine I said, "At least there have been no fatalities, right?"

"Right." There was sorrow in Constantine's gaze. The kind I'd expect to accompany really bad news. I was grateful when he said nothing else.

I exited the house from the back door and rounded the side toward the front porch. Alex wasn't there. I backtracked and checked the other side. Nothing. He wasn't in the shed either.

I could feel panic rising inside me with every minute that passed. "Alex? Where are you?" I called out. Constantine came up behind me. "Can you try his cell phone?" I asked.

"Already on it." He brought the phone to his ear, but a moment later shook his head. "Straight to voicemail."

"Shit. What if he heard us? He must be devastated, thinking he might be the one who hurt those women." I started to take off, but Constantine was next to me in a flash.

He grabbed my forearm and held me in place. "Cherry, there's one possibility we haven't considered."

"What?" I was barely listening, needing to go after Alex immediately, before he did something stupid, or Willoughby found him and decided to finish what he'd started.

Constantine shook me lightly, until I met his gaze. "His actions may not have been subconscious," he said.

"What are you talking about?" I didn't know my voice could be pitched so high. Why was he stalling me? I'd lost Alex before, when my maker had bled him to the brink of death and left him for me to find. I couldn't let it happen again.

"Cherry, there's a chance Alex didn't run because he found out what he's been doing, but because we did."

At first, I couldn't wrap my mind around the meaning of Constantine's words. Then it slowly sank in. "You think he's been hunting and keeping it from us on purpose? No. You didn't see him in the woods. I did." And I'd seen him smile when he'd said I loved him. I hadn't liked that smile.

"This does not mean there isn't more you don't know. Have you wondered why Willoughby bothered following us here, instead of making a move while we were all tucked away in the mansion?"

"I… No."

"I have. And why did Alex insist to meet your folks, when he hasn't spent one minute since we arrived trying to get to know them?"

"He talked to my mom. We've all been busy. What are you getting at?" I tapped my foot impatiently.

"Maybe he's aware of his actions. I'm not suggesting he's gone rogue. Perhaps Willoughby has gotten to him somehow. I don't know… I just want you to be caref—"

"*No.*" I shook off his hold and narrowed my eyes. Fear sliced through me, at the thought he might be right. Alex might be hurting people consciously. Wanting to hurt me.

I don't like being afraid. I hate the helpless feeling that comes with it. The unease in my stomach. The uncertainty. The despair. So I did what I do best with emotions that make me uncomfortable, and funneled it into anger. "I knew you weren't as cool with Alex as you pretended to be, but this is really low. Pretending to worry about me? Saying maybe he's working with Willoughby?"

"Not because he wants to. There have been stories in the past of vampires messing with other vampires' minds. And you should be careful around him. It can't be a coincidence that he targets women who look like you." He reached for me again, but I pushed him back.

"Maybe he thinks he's feeding on me when he attacks them, *because he always feeds on me*." I refused to believe Alex would do these things consciously, or that he'd be a danger to me.

But he'd lied about the dream.

And he'd been weird.

"Or maybe there's another reason," Constantine said, and I was furious at him again, for making me doubt Alex's sincerity. Alex's love for me.

"Right," I said. "He subconsciously wants to drain me, while you only want what's best for me. Is that it?"

"Cherry, I'm only trying to protect you."

"Weird, 'cause I remember feeling pretty fucking devastated, when I caught you screwing someone else. The same someone who had me killed. Maybe you could have tried to protect me then."

Shock and hurt contorted his beautiful face, and a numbing cold spread inside my chest, but I didn't stick around to hear what he said next.

Chapter Sixteen

Alex wasn't in the woods. I know, because I spent five hours looking for him there. I flew over it and I hurtled through it, and I almost got shot when I scared one of San Luis's finest, patrolling the area in the middle of the night. I didn't have the time to play Scared Tourist Lost, so I compelled him enough to make him look the other way, while I fled toward the town center.

I revisited every place we'd checked for Willoughby, and even went by the hospital, where I was told my sort-of-lookalike had been released.

Asking about a patient whose name you don't know has to be hard when you're not a vampire. All I did was use my vampire gaze to get one of the nurses on shift to tell me about the redhead they'd found near the creek, before I deleted all signs of me from her memory.

A bit after six in the morning, I returned to the house, to see if Constantine had had any luck.

I ran into my mom at the door. Shit. Last she'd heard from me, I was joining her and dad for dessert.

"*Mom.* I'm so sorry about last night. We—"

"Don't worry, hon. Constantine explained someone called about… that man"—she spat the words out—"and you went to investigate."

She waved one hand dismissively, and I finally realized she really had no idea about the sort of monster Willoughby was. She might have seen her mother nearly killed by a vampire, but she expected Alex, Constantine, and me to defeat Willoughby. For her it was a matter of time.

I also realized Constantine didn't want to worry her with Alex's disappearance. I'd follow his example.

"Did you find anything?" Mom asked.

I shook my head. "I was hoping Constantine may have heard something more, since… since Alex and I went looking."

"He left shortly after you did. Said he would check out the local nightclubs." She gave me a cheeky grin. "I'm not sure if he's looking for Willoughby or a good time."

So Constantine had stuck with his insane theory. While I'd been looking for a guilt-ridden Alex, my ex had been searching for a hunting one.

I forced my lips to mirror Mom's expression, while inside I seethed with anger. If I were human, my temples would be throbbing. I wanted to bust Constantine's stubborn head as much as I wanted to bust Alex's inconsiderate one.

Maybe I should smash them together. Then they'd both stop messing with my peace of mind.

"You may be right," I said. "I'll rest a little before going back out. What are you up to, so early in the morning?"

She reached for a woven bag she'd left at the doorstep, and held out a pair of pruning scissors. "I promised Ms. Wilkins to help her with her gardening. She was so kind, when we thought you weren't coming back, and I like helping her. If you need company, I can call her—"

"No." I shook my head. "Go. I'll probably sleep for an hour and then meet up with the guys."

"If you're sure." She kissed my forehead.

"I am." It'd be easier for me to scurry around, if I didn't have to hide my panic. I watched her head out, wondering what she'd tell Ms. Wilkins about my return.

I'd find out soon enough. Now I needed to feed, and possibly sleep for an hour or so. No longer than that. I couldn't let more time pass by than absolutely necessary.

Constantine returned alone too. He avoided my gaze. I didn't speak to him. It was two hours after dawn, and I was wild with fear.

Alex could be anywhere.

With every minute that ticked by, I forgot I'd ever been upset with him. Worry gnawed at my unbeating heart. Last time I waited for him for hours, it was because he was dying.

No. This time was different. He was somewhere moping, but reason would overcome his horror of what he might have done, and he'd be back soon. When there was no sign of him by half past ten, I went looking again. I couldn't fly this time, because my vision was blurry with tears. I wouldn't be able to handle it, if something else happened to Alex only because he had the misfortune of knowing me.

I stayed out until the heat became near-unbearable. Only it wasn't in an *oh-God-I'm-burning* way. More like I needed a cold drink and a thick layer of sunscreen. Even so, it was too much after I'd spent years in the night.

I went home for a shower and another hit of blood with Ruby's brew, and was about to brave the bright outdoors again, when Alex sauntered into the living room.

"Isn't the sun amazing?" he asked. "Hadn't realized how much I'd missed it." He wore his best boyish grin, but his eyes held a near-wolfish glint.

I threw myself in his arms. "You're okay. *God.* You don't know how worried I was."

He pulled back. "Why?" He seemed genuinely confused.

I smacked his shoulder, possibly a tad harder than would be playful. "You left without a word and stayed out all night. And then, this morning, you could have burned to ash."

He circled my waist with one arm and nipped at my throat. "I was careful. And I'm perfectly fine, as you can see."

He raised his head and smiled as I looked up. He was more than fine. He was glowing with health and looked better than ever. I sniffed the air around him and had to cover a shocked gasp with my hand, when the familiar sweet and coppery scent hit my nostrils.

"You fed." I tried to keep my voice emotionless. Really, I did.

He pinned me with his sharp gaze, his grey eyes holding none of their usual softness. "Is that a problem? I thought you wanted me to."

I did, but in a controlled environment. Preferably controlled by me. "I did. I do. But you were completely against it. What changed your mind?"

He gave me a one-shouldered shrug and grazed the top of my breasts with the fingertips of his free hand. "Not sure. I felt like trying something different. Maybe you're right. Maybe I should embrace my new lease on life and not try to hang on to the human I used to be."

I shivered. That didn't sound half as cool as it had when I'd suggested it.

"Maybe I should become more like Cee," Alex said, between kissing my neck and nuzzling my hair. "He seems to have a good grasp on things."

"What did you do?" I tried to step back and look him in the eye, but he tightened his hold and swayed us from side to side. "He seems to still have a good grasp on you, too." His words made a mockery of the lovers' dance he was leading our feet on.

I pushed at his chest hard enough to get free. "What did you do?" I repeated.

"Went for a walk and had a bite. What's gotten you all riled up?"

I searched his eyes, hoping to find them blurry. It'd all be better if he was in some kind of trance. They were clear, but shone feverishly.

"Who did you feed on?" I asked. "Were they on drugs?"

He smacked his lips. "I sincerely doubt it. She looked clean cut. A good girl, all in all."

She. My gut clenched. "Where is she now?"

"Left her where I found her." He arched a dark eyebrow. "Breathing, before you ask."

"Did you wipe her memory?"

"No, but she never saw my face, and I doubt anyone will believe her, if she starts talking about vampires."

I winced, both at his callous indifference and at the thought of what I should ask next. "Alex, was she a redhead?"

"Don't remember. What if she was?" His expression, already distant, turned stony.

"Alex, look at me."

He did, crossing his arms. "What am I supposed to see?"

I chewed on the inside of my cheek. "Did you overhear my conversation with Constantine last night?"

"Why? Do you two have secrets?" He narrowed his eyes, his full lips a thin white line.

"No. Nothing like that. I was telling him you haven't been yourself lately. After you walked in the woods… You may be doing things in your sleep that you don't remember afterward." I paused, extremely uncomfortable at what we needed to discuss. How do you tell the man you love you believe he's turning into a monster in his sleep? "Perhaps you're feeling some resentment toward me. Your subconscious could be blaming me for your death, and this is how your id is acting on it. Or whatever."

His expression softened. "Cherry, I love you. I'm not blaming you for anything. Willoughby killed me; you just showed me another way to live." He cupped my neck, and I raised my face to him. "As long as I know you love me, I'm happy," he whispered against my lips, before claiming them for a kiss.

He used one hand to bring me flush against his body, and then drove it downward, until he was kneading my ass. "Want to go downstairs?" he asked between kisses.

I nodded and nuzzled his cheek. I was anything but horny, but needed the connection sex established between us. "I'll let Constantine know you're back."

"You're telling him a lot lately. Have you also told him about my nightmares? About the time I got confused? In bed?"

He meant when he'd attacked me in his sleep. When he'd hurt me. When he'd attacked me in his sleep. Unease sent ice gliding down my spine at the memory of being unable to fight back. The need to connect turned into the imperative to distance myself.

I gulped, but schooled my features to remain placid. "That's between you and me, and it's in the past. He's out looking for you, and I don't want him accidentally walking in on us when he comes back."

Moving behind me, Alex slid his palm to my throat, and then down to my breast. He tweaked my nipple, where it stretched the cotton of my top. "We could stay right here and try to be fast," he whispered in my ear, pressing his erection in my back. His voice was sweet, but dark and sticky, and with a bitter undertone, like burnt caramel.

"You're crazy. Mom or Constantine may show up any second now."

"Then we better get to it." He slid his hand inside my jeans and pressed at my clit over my panties, grinding his hips against me. "You're already wet."

I usually was, around him. My body reacted to his touch instinctively. I rocked against him for a moment, before gathering my wits and stilling his wrist. "Alex, no. Let me make this phone call, and we can go where we'll have some privacy."

He managed to move my underwear aside and slip a finger inside me. "You mean where your precious Constantine won't see and get jealous."

His words stunned me long enough for him to add a second finger.

"Maybe he should watch." He pumped the fingers inside me and palmed my breast. "Maybe he likes to watch. Maybe he'll finally realize you're mine."

A moan reached my ears. My moan. I shouldn't be doing this here. I shouldn't be doing this at all. There was something wrong with Alex, and I wasn't letting his sexiness distract me from it. I pulled his hand out and squeezed my thighs together. "This is ridiculous. He and I have been over for years. He knows I'm with you. I haven't exactly been subtle about it. You go downstairs, and I'll be with you in a sec." I tried to sound seductive, despite the unease making my stomach roil.

He shrugged and licked his fingers clean. "If you're not down in two, I'm coming to get you." His nonchalance would have pissed me off, if I weren't already busy being worried sick.

I watched him swagger toward the basement entrance, and then typed a text to Constantine. I wasn't going to risk Alex's overhearing what I wanted to say.

Alex is back. You may be right. If you say I told you so, UR dead. Come home now. And plz interrupt.

"You coming?" Alex yelled.

"Be right there." I infused my words with a throaty sultriness I didn't feel.

The front door flew open, and Constantine entered. He gave off a vibe I wasn't used to, but I couldn't spot what was different about him.

Not knowing with the fuck was wrong with my guys was becoming a trend lately.

"You're back," I said for Alex to hear.

"I am. Is Alex well?" Constantine's blue eyes asked if I was all right.

I shook my head. "He's fine, thank God. He even fed." I widened my eyes, hoping he understood the last bit of info didn't make me as happy as I pretended to be.

Constantine frowned. "That's good to hear. And everything went smoothly? How did he decide to take that step?"

"You can ask the man yourself," Alex said from behind me.

I turned and watched him approach in long, slow strides. He only had his jeans on, their top button popped, letting them hang low on his hips.

"It was about time I lost my training wheels. And yes, everything went smoothly," he said, stopping next to me. He wrapped an arm around my waist and gathered me to his side a little more forcefully than necessary. "And now we know we're all well, you'll excuse us, Cee." He pulled me backward, and I threw Constantine a glance I hoped conveyed how much I didn't want to be alone with Alex right then.

If I had to, I was prepared to fight Alex off, but I preferred to avoid violence and get to the root of the problem.

Constantine didn't miss a beat. "I'm afraid your little reunion will have to wait." He might be a lot of things—conceited self-serving bastard topping that list more often than not—but he wasn't stupid. "As a council member, I'm afraid I am required by law to debrief you after your first feeding. I need to know who she was." He tilted his head and studied Alex's face. "I assume she was a she?"

Alex nodded, and Constantine went on. "Where you found her; how you approached her; how many pints you imbibed; what condition you left her in; what precautions you took to protect your identity and our kind. We must address all those issues and make sure you didn't cross any lines with the locals."

"Everything is fine. I found her in a coffee shop near the university, and she was alive and still standing last I saw her. This can wait." Alex caressed the length of my arm down to my wrist and tangled his fingers with mine. "Let's go, Cherry."

"You're going nowhere until I get answers." I don't believe I'd ever seen Constantine so serious or so commanding before. It was like he'd unfolded to a height even taller than his six-feet-three. His square shoulders appeared carved in stone, and his voice boomed. "I am the one who allows your continued existence, against vampire law. I am risking everything by keeping you hidden from the council. In my home, nonetheless. You *will* tell me how you spent the hours we wasted looking for you, and you will hope none of it displeases me."

Alex matched Constantine's posture, his own chest puffed. For what felt like an eternity, they stood there, staring each other down. Despite their similar height and Alex's being at least ten pounds heavier, it was soon apparent he wasn't going to win this match. Constantine's gaze was pure steel, forged through the centuries, while Alex's was iron. Hard but brittle.

And he broke.

I could tell the moment he decided to concede, from the way his body relaxed, his back slumping the smallest fraction of an inch, his eyes mellowing. He hooked his thumbs through his belt loops, not so inadvertently pulling the jeans even lower, until I could almost see where the happy trail that began under his navel ended.

"Okay," he said. "I guess Cherry will have to wait a little longer. Let me give her something to tide her over."

Before either I or Constantine could react, Alex dipped me backward and gave me the mother of all Hollywood kisses.

If I were in the mood, the kiss would have *really* gotten me in the mood. Now it felt awkward and stilted, and too much like a show for my ex's sake.

If it was actually meant to upset Constantine, it didn't work. He didn't even bat an eyelash. "And now that's settled, let her get some sleep. She must be exhausted after looking for you for this long." He motioned for Alex to enter the kitchen ahead of him.

I saw Constantine type something on his phone as he followed. A second later, my own cell buzzed in my pocket. A text from him.

Are you all right?

I replied, my thumb flying on the virtual keypad.

Scared. And still hoping you're wrong.

He threw me a smile over his shoulder and typed something else before leaving my line of sight.

I'll take that as an apology.

He closed the door behind them, leaving me to my mostly unpleasant thoughts.

Chapter Seventeen

It took only the minimum amount of effort for me to convince myself listening in on Alex and Constantine was a good idea.

I stretched out on the living-room couch, eyes shut. If anyone walked in, or barged out of the kitchen in a huff, I would appear to be asleep. In truth, I adjusted my hearing until I made out the soft sound of sneakers dragging along the kitchen floor.

Alex pacing, probably. He'd seemed more agitated than Constantine.

"Where did you go when you first left the house?" Constantine asked.

"For a walk. It was a starry night. I thought I'd let the romantic in me roam free." Sarcasm laced Alex's reply.

"What made you leave in the first place? Kathleen said your mother was on the phone. Did something happen?"

"Do you really care about all that, or are you trying to keep me away from Cherry? Like with the sparring?"

"We've already had this conversation. Repeatedly. I thought the last time I broke your nose you finally believed I wasn't after her."

My eyes flew open. So that was what their antagonism had been about back at the mansion. Alex had openly accused Constantine of trying to get between us. And a broken nose, more than once? Sure, it was nothing for a vampire, and I got why Alex wouldn't want to tell me about his stupid jealousy, but why hadn't Constantine said something? That was one twisted sense of male solidarity.

"I have no reason to keep you and Cherry apart. I wouldn't have offered you my hospitality if your relationship bothered me." Constantine's tone was impatient more than reassuring. "Why is it you think the worst of me? Nothing would have been easier than getting rid of you, back when you were human. Or during your turning. I did not have to bring you back to the mansion, when I found you freshly turned. I didn't have to come for you at all.

"Cherry wouldn't have known if I... took care of things. She was so distraught when she found you half drained by Willoughby, she thought feeding you her blood hadn't worked. I could have told her you didn't make it through the change. I took you in when I didn't have to. I am training you, to ensure you can survive in a fight against others of our kind. I even disregarded the council and allowed you and Cherry to meet each other's parents. You should know you can trust me by now."

"For her. You did all of that for Cherry, not 'cause you're my friend," Alex whispered.

Constantine lowered his voice, until I had trouble making out the words. "Of course I did. I would do anything for her, and that includes becoming a true friend to you. Now stop being a child, and tell me why you left last night."

Unbidden thoughts invaded my mind during the pause that followed. Constantine would do anything for me. I knew that already, though, didn't I? Everything he'd told Alex was true. Constantine didn't have to save Alex from walking in the sun when he first awoke as a dazed, disoriented fledgling. Didn't have to feed him his own blood to help regain his strength. Didn't have to put us both up and watch us be happy together.

Assuming Alex and I could still be happy. Or together.

What seemed like a lifetime ago, when Alex was human and Constantine was the man who betrayed me, my ex played the long game—allowing me to be with Alex for however long that lasted. Now he had nothing to gain, but still he helped me.

"I left because I felt suffocated." Alex's voice fished me out of that downward spiral. "My mother was asking about Cherry's family and when I'd pop the question, and all I thought about was Cherry's words in the woods. How we can never have a family. I don't want a family, but I have to explain it to the woman expecting grandkids from me. And then she asked when I'm going back to work, and I don't fucking know that either. I needed some space, so I left."

"So you left. Without a word. When you knew Willoughby was out there." Constantine's skepticism didn't surprise me. Alex's excuse would have worked if I'd used it, since I tended to flee when faced with things I didn't like. But he was usually the one who attacked problems headfirst.

"I wasn't thinking," Alex said.

"I find that hard to believe. You've been trained to think. You think for a living."

"Yeah, well, I snapped, okay?" As he did now, his answer loud enough to carry, even if I weren't using my vampire hearing.

"Where did you find the girl?" Constantine asked.

It took me a second to follow that change in subject, but Alex was faster. "A coffee place. Didn't notice the name. She stood alone by the restrooms, watching a group of students laugh and talk. I pretended to go to the little boys' room, then doubled back and grabbed her from behind. I whispered in her ear that I'd kill her if she made a sound, and she let me pull her into one of the stalls. She never saw my face. I drank until she was weak. Her heart was still beating. Told her to keep staring at the wall until ten minutes passed, and I left. I didn't risk us. Satisfied?"

A shiver ran down my spine at his dispassionate account of how he'd threatened, scared, and fed on a young woman who'd done nothing to him. He'd sworn to serve and protect people like her, and until recently couldn't have entertained the idea of sinking his fangs into anyone but me.

What happened to him?

"Was she a redhead?" Constantine asked.

Alex snorted. "I don't know. Wasn't paying attention to her hair."

"Really? Was it short? Pulled back? Didn't you have to get it out of the way to reach her throat? You'd think its color would have registered."

"It didn't."

"All right." Constantine sighed.

"Are we done?"

"Not quite."

"What else do you need to know? If I enjoyed it? How warm her blood felt on my tongue, compared to Cherry's?

I was done. I didn't want to hear how he'd felt, drinking from someone else—if he'd gotten hard, like he always did when he fed on me.

The rational part of me reminded me how much more potent vampire blood was. Humans were warm and soft and yielding, but their essence didn't pack the zing ours did. It didn't provide the rush Alex felt every time he drank from me. Human blood wasn't as thick, or as infused with power.

But it tasted different every time.

Before Alex had been killed by my maker, I'd tried to explain to him what it felt like feeding from him. I said it was like licking my favorite treat—chocolate fudge—from his naked body. I could never get bored of it.

It didn't mean he saw things the same way.

This thought process was driving me crazy, and there was no room for more craziness in my existence. Willoughby had to be dealt with, and we needed to get to the bottom of whatever was eating at Alex. My relationship issues could wait. If I'd learned anything the past few months, was how to prioritize.

Sometimes I even practiced what I'd learned, and for now, my priority should be to clear my head and relax. Perhaps catch up on sleep.

Every fiber in my stupid body said I needed to confront Alex, though. I had to tell him my—*Constantine's* theory and force him to come clean. Whatever he'd done, we'd deal with together. There were no fatalities. No permanent damage. He hadn't exposed us.

We could come back from this.

Assuming Alex wanted to.

The iciness in his voice earlier, the lack of emotion in his gaze when he'd told me he'd fed, the way he'd responded to Constantine's questions—all indicated whatever had gotten hold of him had sunk its claws in deep. A confrontation wouldn't help, until I knew what we were dealing with.

If it was an external factor, and not some previously hidden side of Alex now rearing its ugly head.

How well did I really know him? We'd only met a little over two months ago, even if it felt like years with everything that transpired in the meantime. He could very well have always harbored a mean streak. A shadowy self that enjoyed hurting others and getting away with it.

Maybe a side that enjoyed hurting me.

Could his darkness be mere jealousy? How far back did he begin changing? How did I not notice?

For the first time since I began suspecting something wasn't right with my lover, I thought of how he'd looked at me when I woke up to him having sex with me. The way he'd taken me in the shed. The way his eyes had clouded when he'd thought he had good reason to be upset with me or Constantine. What Sheena had told me about him and Constantine duking it out back at the mansion. It could all be connected.

It *was* all connected.

My stomach plummeted, and my head felt light. How hadn't I realized it?

And when did it start?

When Alex and I first hooked up, he said he'd had a bad relationship in the past, with someone who couldn't take his way of life. He told me he didn't want to fall for someone who had baggage, and I promised him Constantine wouldn't be an issue.

Did I lie?

Since my breakup with Constantine, I didn't allow myself to consider getting back together with him. And now I was with Alex, I would never think of returning to my ex. Despite knowing the end of our relationship had been choreographed by his maker.

That didn't change anything.

Neither did the realization Constantine truly loved me and always had, even when he cheated on me. He believed what I thought was a cheap excuse—that eternity is too long to spend it monogamously, and sex has nothing to do with feelings.

It wasn't an entirely crazy theory. Who knew how I'd feel if I'd been around as long as he had?

Nope. I wasn't going there.

I was in love with Alex.

But my assurances obviously didn't suffice. He became more possessive by the day, gradually losing the gentleness and stability I'd come to love. Jealousy shouldn't have been enough for him to start attacking women out of the blue, though. Not enough for him to be so rough with me—and the more I thought about it, the more his roughness seemed a display of power, and not a manifestation of his uncontrollable lust for me.

If I was to keep my sanity, I had to believe there was more there. I had to believe Willoughby was somehow involved. That Alex's Mr. Hyde wasn't coming to play. I needed someone to tell me whether vampires could control each other's mind. I couldn't be sure Constantine would have let on, if he knew anything more than the rumor he mentioned, but he'd have taken advantage of it a lot sooner. Possibly to convince me to forgive his betrayal. Pity my grandma was in Europe. Judging by the filter she'd concocted, she knew things your garden-variety vampire didn't.

A door slamming shut brought me back to reality. Moments later, my mom was there, arms laden with groceries.

"Hey." I stood to greet her, wondering what store was open in town in the middle of the night. Oh, wait. I was up in the middle of the *day*. In a sunlit room.

I stole a moment to bask in the glow, and promised myself I'd be going on that picnic with Alex as soon as we'd figured things out.

"Are the boys home?" Mom asked. "Any news on Willoughby?"

There was no reason to worry her. There were enough of us losing sleep over the whole situation. "They're both back, but we got nothing on Willoughby. Alex was out till now. He decided to test the potion." I spread my arms in the sunlight. "As you can see, it works." I forced a smile as I took most of the bags, and then waited for her to open the door to the kitchen. I wasn't crazy about the idea of facing the men in there, but I wouldn't be a refugee in my childhood home.

Mom arched both eyebrows. "He was out till now? It's past noon. Next time he decides to check if something works, maybe he should do so in less lethal conditions." She spoke loudly on purpose, to make sure Alex picked up the admonition.

"You're absolutely right, Kathleen. I was too excited and didn't think." Alex sounded contrite, but I didn't buy it.

"All's well that ends well." She rinsed her hands in the kitchen sink, wiped them on a dishtowel, and set the electric pot on, before ducking out again.

Fixing my faux smile in place, I ignored the conversation behind me, made a beeline for the fridge, and began unloading cans and bottles.

Mom's process was one of the things that had mercifully remained unchanged by time. She put on the kettle for tea, and left to change into house clothes and shoes, before starting on lunch. This was my chance to talk to her alone.

"Whatcha making?" I asked in my cutest voice, as soon as she was back, in her yoga pants and extra large T-shirt. Alex and Constantine had been eerily silent, and I wanted them out of the kitchen and to a place where they could safely stop repressing their grievances, before they exploded.

"I was thinking of pasta with fresh tomato and basil sauce. Did you have something else in mind?"

I shook my head, studying Alex's stony expression and Constantine's stiff posture out the corner of my eye. "I can help. For old times' sake. Maybe start with peeling the tomatoes?"

Mom grinned, and the years slid off her, until she was the thirty year old who tucked me in when I was a little girl. "I've missed that," she said and tilted her head toward the tomatoes neatly piled in the top shelf of the kitchen trolley. "You better get started, if you want actual lunch today."

"And maybe the guys could spend that time sparring?" Somewhere far, far away from mortals, if possible.

For the first time since I entered the kitchen, I turned to them. Alex still appeared impassive, while Constantine gave me a speculative look.

"If Willoughby is planning an attack, we all need to be at our best," I said. "He's older than all of us. I know I can't win in a fair fight with him, but you both could improve your chances with some training. You could use the back yard."

Constantine nodded. "I wouldn't mind some playtime in the sun. Alex, are you up for it?"

Alex stood, all but kicking his chair back. "Going to wipe the floor with you, old man." The words were playful, but his tone wasn't.

"Have some more of the potion first?" Mom glanced at me as she spoke to them. I gave a tiny shrug. Surprisingly, she said nothing until we were alone.

Until the very moment we were alone.

The door was still ajar when she mouthed, "What was that?"

I held up a palm and waited until I heard heavy footsteps tread down the porch steps, before telling her of the suspicions Constantine and I shared.

She sank in a chair, waved me to the one next to her, and listened in rapt fascination, while I detailed the instances on which Alex allowed me glimpses of a man I barely recognized.

"So you're saying something may be driving him literally mad with jealousy?" she asked when I was done.

"But in a weird, exaggerated way. If you could see his eyes… I can literally see him transform into someone else."

"You think it's something paranormal." It wasn't a question.

"It's either that, or he's always been this way and didn't have time to show it before. I don't want to believe it, Mom. You don't know how kind he is."

"He's been nothing but a perfect gentleman to me and your father. To you too, as far as I know. If he's laid a hand on you, I'll be really disappointed in him." Her gaze was so hard, she might as well have said she'd shower him with acid. For a moment I could believe she'd kick his ass if she believed he'd hurt me. She certainly looked as ferocious as a momma bear whose cub was facing a threat.

"He hasn't. He wouldn't. I'll tell you if he does." I winked, hoping it reassured her.

"Good. Now what are you going to do about it? How can you find out for sure what's causing this? And are you still waiting for Willoughby to come to you, or are you going after him?"

I shrugged. "We still don't have a plan, and we can't come up with one until we know we can count on Alex not to flip sides. I guess Constantine and I could try going after Willoughby without Alex, but I'd rather keep a close eye on him at all times."

"And you won't know what he'll do until you figure out what's happening to him."

"Exactly. Which is why I wanted to ask you if Ruby ever said something about vampires practicing mind control?"

Mom looked at me questioningly. "I thought you already knew. Don't they teach newbies anything these days?"

I felt a tingle of hope before I realized she'd misunderstood. "I mean controlling other vampires, not humans."

She furrowed her brow. Beside her, the pile of unpeeled tomatoes mocked us. If we didn't get started soon, we wouldn't be on time.

Which seemed to apply to everything as of late.

"Nothing?" I asked her. "Does she have some sort of diary? Notes? Something on the PC maybe." Light-bulb moment. "Where did she write the recipe for the daylight potion?"

Mom shook her head. "She doesn't trust anyone with the recipe. Once she perfected it, she destroyed all her notes on it. She has no files on this computer—only her laptop, and that's with her."

No luck there, then. "Damn it. I was hoping for precedence of vampires being controlled in their sleep. Guess it was a long shot."

"Oh, wait." Mom jumped up, and my unbeating heart leapt in my chest. "I remember Ruby saying she had the weirdest dream, soon after we moved to the States. Constantine came to her, to check if we were okay. She told him he couldn't really be there, and he said he'd tasted her blood, so all he had to do was go to sleep focusing on her. It was all very surreal for her. I didn't think of it sooner, because she had no doubt her imagination had made the whole thing up. But maybe…"

My eyes felt about to bug out of my head. If that was the case, could Constantine visit the dreams of anyone whose blood he'd tasted? Would they know if he did?

Would *I* know?

That was a question for another day. "Could there be more you don't remember? Maybe if I hypnotized you?"

"No, I'm not forgetting anything. Now that I recalled the conversation, it's as clear as if we had it yesterday. You should ask Constantine for details. If he was really there, he'll know."

I didn't want to ask him. I'd have to ask why he didn't say anything sooner, and that would only lead to badness.

"I think I'll try it myself," I told Mom. "See how that goes. Can you please not mention anything for now?"

She nodded. "But honey, if you need help, you can ask him. I trust him completely."

So did I, which was scary, because he wasn't a paragon of honesty. If he didn't lie, he withheld the truth. The end result was the same.

The men returned for lunch, and then disappeared again. Not that I minded. It gave me more time to figure out how to emulate what my mother said Constantine could do.

From what Mom said, Constantine had simply focused on Ruby at the right moment. I fell asleep thinking of Alex more than once, but I never landed in his dream, so I guessed it worked the same way flying did. We had to believe we could do it, and will ourselves to follow through.

Tonight I didn't feel like sleeping next to Alex. My skin prickled at the thought of him touching me, making love to me, when he felt like a complete stranger. I lay staring at the ceiling, as he came out of the shower, and I kept my gaze from diverting to what the towel around his hips left uncovered. Namely, most of his amazing body. Not looking straight at him didn't help. Even if his wide shoulders didn't butt into my peripheral vision, I knew by heart every inch of his hard pecs and cut stomach, sprinkled with a dusting of dark hair.

I was generally happy my hormones hadn't died when I did, but that moment, they mainly pissed me off.

Luckily, Alex passed out the moment he hit the mattress. Constantine had worn him out thoroughly. Or maybe it was the excitement of the day, and he'd wake up rested and back to himself in the morning. If wishes were horses…

I needed my beauty sleep, but my body wasn't yet used to my return to a human time schedule, despite my exhaustion.

Also, trying to find a way to spy on my lover, in case my maker had him under a spell, wasn't really conducive to relaxing enough to fall asleep.

Fun.

Not.

If I didn't fall asleep I couldn't enter Alex's dreamland—assuming I'd even manage to if I did sleep.

I got comfy on my back and threw one arm over my eyes, trying to focus on all that was good and kind about Alex. All that I loved about him. I needed to remember these things anyway, whether my plan worked or not. For my sake.

Our first night together. He initially thought I was a prostitute, and invited me home for a lecture, instead of the naughty times I had in mind. The naughty times were had after all, and what enraged me at the time was now our private joke.

He was always so open. So willing to talk about his feelings. So ready to trust me. To love me. To make me his priority. My chest expanded with the love I felt for him.

He'd stuck with me after he'd seen me sprout fangs. After he'd found out my true nature. He loved me despite losing his life as punishment for being my lover.

He introduced me to his mother.

He—

He sat on the same log, in the same clearing. In front of me.

I was asleep.

And inside Alex's dream.

Chapter Eighteen

The sensation of peace is all encompassing. No. All pervasive.

It's an unnatural peace. Forced.

Alex sits in the sun, only a handful of feet away. I could reach him in a human heartbeat, but my feet are cemented in place. My inability to move doesn't scare me. It somehow matches the tranquility of the forest.

Utter tranquility. Disturbing.

No wind rustling the leaves. No birds chirping. No wildlife whatsoever. It's like nature is in a coma. Makes sense Alex doesn't spend time recreating forest sounds in his sleep, but everything else seems a perfect copy of reality.

He raises his gaze, and I suck in a breath when he looks straight at me.

"You came." The smile on his lips is the exact same I saw when I followed him to this very clearing in real life.

What? He expected me?

Before I can ask, a female voice comes from right behind me. "How could I not? You know how I feel about you."

I know this voice. Where do I know this voice from?

I try to turn, to see who spoke, but I'm rooted in place. Worse, I have absolutely no control over my body.

A burst of cold spreads through me, from my chest outward, tying my stomach into a knot, making my throat clench, and numbing my fingers. It's gone as suddenly as it appeared, and I'm left looking at the back of a blonde head. The figure in front of me gradually comes into better focus and assumes shape as it nears Alex, adding to the distance between us.

A thick blonde braid draped over one shoulder. An almost bare back, pale and smooth. Voluptuous hips, swathed in barely-there strips of see-through gauze.

Ádísa. This figure can't belong to anyone else.

Why is Alex dreaming of her? He only saw her that one night, when she tried to kill all three of us. Constantine ripped her head off and turned her to dust, but she apparently had plenty of time to make an impression on Alex by then.

We certainly talked about her a lot lately. Alex's subconscious is probably messing with him.

I realize she must have passed through me. Was that the cold I felt all the way to my core?

If this is Alex's dream, how can the image of Ádísa bring forth a physical reaction in me?

She reaches him and sinks down to her knees by his side. "I'll always come to you. Always put you first." She trails a hand up his… calf? I can't really see from where I stand.

"Can you say the same for Cherry?" she asks.

Sick to my stomach, I wait to hear his response.

"Cherry loves me."

Is this some weird déjà vu? A replay of whatever he was dreaming when he sleepwalked? This is the time to check if I'm doing this right. Ruby was able to see Constantine when he shared her dream.

"Yes, Alex"—I smile—"I do love you. I'm here. Can you hear me?"

He doesn't bat an eyelash or look at me. His face is turned to hers, but from what I can make out, he's still smiling.

The clarity of the dream strikes me. I've never dreamed in such detail. My gaze is drawn to the blue sapphire gleaming on the cleft of my arch enemy's throat.

Details. Not as important as what Ádísa is busying herself with. And she's undoing Alex's pants. She makes herself comfortable between his thighs and pushes her hand inside the opening of his jeans.

I gag. "Alex, I'm here. Stop her. Send her away."

Still no sign he hears me. His eyes drift shut, and his head rolls back.

The bitch meets my gaze, and the look she gives me is the same as when I caught Constantine and her in bed together.

Triumphant.

She feels triumphant. In Alex's dream.

Something is even more wrong than I suspected.

I sense another presence, and again try to look behind me but can't move. This one isn't threatening—I don't think. It's just there.

Always looking at me, Ádísa licks her lips. "Does she appreciate you like I do, Alex?" She raises his shirt and kisses his navel. Alex moans. "Would she put you above everyone else?" Her sharp nails leave red lines on his side. "Even Constantine?"

"Cherry loves me." Alex stills her moves, and I silently squeal in delight. Then I realize he hasn't removed her hands from his body.

It's a dream. Just a dream. I can't be jealous of a dream. Even if it's of the woman who destroyed my life and was the reason Alex lost his.

"But does she love you enough?" Ádísa asks. "I would love you enough. You could fix it, if you did what I told you. Then you could have it all."

What? What did she tell him to do? It feels important.

So many things are important, but I can't tell why— like that Ádísa is less real than Alex. Less substantial. She's still more solid than I am.

Alex moans. It sounds like he's enjoying himself, and I'm glad Ádísa's hair now hides whatever she's doing to him.

Shit. Is she...?

I can't watch, while she has imaginary oral sex with my boyfriend, and I can't leave him here.

Focusing on my love for him, I shout, "Alex, wake up."

Yeah, that doesn't work. No sound makes it out of my lips.

"Alex." Nothing again.

I close my eyes and scream in my head. "Wake up. Wake up. Wake up."

Nope.

I have to wake up. Now. Eyes open, damn it.

Alex lay on top of me, legs tangled with mine. He was hard against my core.

Hard for her.

I grabbed his shoulders and shook him harshly until he opened his eyes. It wouldn't be fair of me to knee him in the balls over something that ultimately wasn't his fault.

"Bad dream?" I asked.

He rolled to his side and took me with him. "Yes. I'm sorry if I scared you. Wanted to feel you." He caressed my stomach and brought one of my legs over his hip.

"This doesn't seem scared." I pumped my hips against his erection once, and then tilted them so my lower body didn't touch his.

"It was fucked up. I think everything we found out about Ádísa got to me. I dreamed she was trying to convince me you didn't love me, and she was pretty damned persuasive. She tried to seduce me, and I sat there, powerless.

Even enjoying it. But it wasn't me. I didn't control it, Cherry. I'm sorry. You know you're the only one I want."

Relief washed over me that he didn't lie. I held his chin and looked into his eyes. They were open and lucid. He knew it was me in bed with him. As things should be. I arched my neck and rubbed my heel up the back of his thigh. Despite all my fears about what was happening, I needed to feel the closeness that bound us when we made love, and the man in front of me was the lover I trusted, not the madman trying to replace him. Ádísa's memory might have turned him on, but I'd reap the benefits and enjoy the hell out of them.

And I would ignore how petty it was that part of me wanted to make love to Alex so I could one-up her.

"Love you," he mumbled in my hair.

"I love you too." Not like he could control his dreams, right?

I pulled him to me and lay back, so he was covering me once more. He propped himself up on one arm and caressed my face with his free hand. "You're so beautiful," he said. "Perfect."

His voice and gaze held such awe, I almost teared up. He was back. The man who'd made me overlook my decision to never fall from a human was in bed with me, planting butterfly kisses on my lips and eyes. He nuzzled my hair and licked a trail down my neck. I'd gone to bed in a tank top and a pair of boy shorts, and it didn't take long for Alex to find his way inside both. Before I knew it, my top was bunched around my waist, and my shorts were hanging from one ankle.

"Touch me." Alex gently led my hand to his cock.

His long, hard shaft throbbed against my palm. I closed my fingers around it, unable to circle it all, and slid my palm up and down its length—squeezing on the upstroke, the way I knew he liked.

He groaned. Grinded against me. "Just like that."

I kissed his jaw line and pulled his earlobe between my teeth. Nibbled on it. "Tell me what you want," I whispered.

"I want to taste you."

I withdrew my hand and spread my legs wider.

"Not there," he said. "I want your blood."

I wrapped my arms around his neck and folded my legs over his hips, so the head of his cock nudged my entrance. "I thought you fed tonight."

"Nothing tastes like you." He pushed forward slowly, until only the tip was inside me. "Nothing measures up."

His words meant more than I cared to admit. He didn't prefer human blood to mine. He didn't miss the warmth.

I hadn't lost him.

I arched my body, trying to take in more of him.

"I need to taste you," he said again.

I tossed my head back, clearing the hair from my neck and baring my throat to him.

He needed no further invitation to sink inside me to the hilt, just as his fangs sliced into my neck. The euphoria of the double penetration was unsurpassable as always, and I gave into him, allowing him to mold my body to his, prolong my pleasure as he took his. I let him take me and take from me, while I fell off the edge again and again, until I could no longer control my limbs.

"Wow," I murmured when he finally stopped moving inside me. I was so lightheaded, the words fell out in a jumble.

Lightheaded. From blood loss.

He was still pulling on my blood.

"Alex. Stop." I couldn't manage more than a whisper, but I knew he heard. He had to have heard.

Why wasn't he stopping?

"Alex? Baby? You're draining me." This came out on a breath and had no more impact than my previous words had.

I didn't have the strength to even panic properly, let alone push him off me. How much had he drunk? I lay there, feeling my second life slip away like my first had. Only this time, it was at the hands of someone who loved me.

I felt sorrow for Alex. By the time he realized he'd taken far too much, I'd be nothing but ash. That was what happened when we no longer had blood in our veins. The end result was the same as if we'd been staked or decapitated.

He'd be so shocked.

No.

Screw Alex's shock. I loved him, but I wasn't going to spend my last moments of existence lamenting his hurt at causing my ultimate demise. I tried to raise a hand and slap some sense into him, since he wasn't listening, but my fingers barely rose from the sheets, before my arm flopped down numbly.

Fuck.

This was it. This was really it.

Alex's weight lifted off me all at once, as though he flew upward. Which, I realized, he did. He flew in a short arc, before landing across the room with a hollow thud.

"Are you all right?" Constantine's face took up my visual field. He looked worried. Why was he worried?

Right. I was half dead.

And completely naked.

Eh, I couldn't let that bother me.

Constantine was more chivalrous than I gave him credit for. He pulled the covers on top of me even before popping open a vein in his wrist. "Here," he said. "Drink."

The classic cologne he preferred caressed my senses. Tobacco, wood, and leather, with dark, spicy undertones that kick-started my sensory memory. I scrunched my nose. "No. Can't." Drinking from another vampire was too intimate, and he and I weren't at that place anymore, however familiar his scent. Hadn't been in a long while. "We broke up." My voice was no louder than before, but he apparently had no issues making out my words clearly.

And why was my brain glitching? Who cared if we weren't together? The man was trying to save my life. "Never mind," I more mouthed than said, before opening up for what he offered.

God, I'd forgotten how good his blood tasted. I don't know if blood ages like wine, but his was richer, thicker, and more fragrant than Alex's. Not that I spent much time thinking about it after the first few drops touched my tongue. I latched on to his self-inflicted bite and sucked greedily. My eyes slid shut, as I felt strength return to my body with every gulp.

"Of course it's Constantine. It's *always* Constantine," I heard Alex say. A growl vibrated in his chest.

I wanted to tell him he should be thanking my ex instead of being all grumpy about his intervention.

No, I wanted to kick his ass for making that intervention necessary. I was done feeling sorry for Alex and worrying he wasn't all right. Done tiptoeing around his feelings. Whatever was happening to him, he had to be a man about it and come clean, not risk my damned life because he felt too embarrassed to own up to it.

I was, of course, too busy feeding to answer him as he deserved, so I kept scolding him in my head while I focused on the task at hand.

A door slammed shut, and I assumed Alex was having a hissy fit. Whatever. Once I was done here, I was totally giving him a piece of my mind. The guilt trip I'd been on since assisting his turning was now over, thank you very much, and our last stop was Reality Check.

The mattress dipped by my side, and I opened my eyes to Constantine half-lying next to me, propped up on the arm not acting as my feeding tube. He looked even paler than usual.

Shit. Now I was overindulging myself. I took one last, ladylike sip, and licked the wound closed. "Thank you."

"Anytime." Constantine smiled wanly. I could see this had gotten a lot out of him.

"I took too much, didn't I?" I tested my limbs. They all seemed to be in working order again. At least I could bring up my knees and turn to my side, to better look at him.

"That's not it." He used one finger to tuck my hair behind my ear. My bangs fell back in place, as always. What had I been thinking, cutting bangs to shoot a porn flick—sorry, adult movie? At least by dying the day after my visit to the salon, I'd have mostly well-styled hair for as long as I roam this earth.

And I was digressing again. Constantine narrowed his eyes at me. "You're having an internal monologue, aren't you? One of those weird ones."

I shook my head. "I haven't done that in years."

Liar.

Shut up.

"Are you okay to get up?" I asked him, to get out of my own head. I didn't want to kick him out. I just wanted to get to Alex, before he continued on his idiotic path of secretive self destruction.

"Right as rain." Constantine started to get up, but I reached for his hand.

"If it's not that I took too much, then what?"

"Nothing. It has been a while."

I wanted to ask if he meant since he'd fed me or since we'd been in bed together. I kept my mouth shut.

He nodded curtly, as if agreeing with something only he'd heard. "I will be right outside. You get dressed, and we shall speak to Alex together."

If *shall* came to play, things were dire indeed. "I'll be right out. And hey, now I can enter your dreams—or I guess I already could, since I had your blood before." I don't know what possessed me to say that. Did I want to let him know I knew? Was it a half-assed attempt to alleviate some tension?

Whatever it was, it worked to reinstate Constantine's usual posture. He rolled his shoulders and stood in one slow, liquid motion. Watching me, he licked his lips and rolled down the sleeve he'd lifted for my sake. "Who says you ever left them?" he asked in the deep baritone he'd once used to whisper in my ear what he was about to do to me.

I still felt Alex inside me, but my whole body gravitated toward Constantine. It was the result of drinking his blood. No other explanation.

"On second thought"—he cleared his throat—"I will go find Alex and wait for you upstairs. Don't take forever."

I barely had time to say okay, before he was out the door. I was still half naked, when he opened it again.

I had my back to it and was pulling up my jeans. "What did you forget?" I asked, turning around in time to see him dump Alex's prone form on the bed. "Constantine, what did you do?" Not that I could blame him for punching Alex's lights out.

"*Nothing.*" He sounded incredulous. "This is how I found him, on the pullout. If I wanted to finish him off, I wouldn't have brought him to you afterward. What am I? A bloody cat?" Constantine rarely lost his cool enough to curse, and his use of the British curse word would have cracked me up, if it weren't for Alex. Lying on the bed. Apparently unconscious.

I could see nothing wrong with him. No wound. No blood, other than the smear of mine around his lips. "Did you try to wake him?"

"No, my first instinct was to shoulder his weight and parade him around the house."

His sarcasm felt familiar, safe, and allowed me to think of other, more important things. "Will he be all right?"

"You know how it is with us. If we're not dust, it's fixable."

I nodded. "I have to go back in," I said.

"Excuse me?"

"His dream. Before he…"

"Yes?" The single word brimmed with impatience.

"Before you stopped Alex, I followed him into his dream. Ádísa was there, and"—I huffed—"I think she was about to blow him."

One corner of Constantine's mouth tagged upward, and I saw his effort to rein in the smile threatening to blossom on his lips. "Not to speak ill of the dead, but she tended to do that to people a lot," he finally said.

Yeah, it was so nice having his usual, cocky self around, instead of the kind, understanding one. Only not. "She was *trying* to get him to say he'd leave me for her. I think that's what she wanted. There was something he had to do, and then he'd have it all, as she put it."

Constantine's eyes lost their playfulness, and his mouth hardened. "What did he say?"

"He kept repeating that I love him, but she was feeding into his jealousy of you." I rolled my eyes. "Yeah, okay, it's no secret he's jealous of you. With no reason whatsoever, I might add."

His smile was no longer suppressed. "Of course. Please, do go on."

"Not much to say. I woke him up before things escalated between them, and he said he must've been affected by all the talking about Ádísa."

"It is a possibility."

Memories of the dream kept coming back to me. "But it was somehow more than that. It seemed like she could see me, when he couldn't. I need to go back in, see if I can talk some sense to him there."

"You said he couldn't see you."

"Yes, but this time you'll tell me how it's done. The right way."

Chapter Nineteen

Constantine paced the length of the room. Repeatedly. It was becoming annoying and didn't let me relax enough to sleep. Let alone how disconcerting it was seeing him stressed. The man was usually cool as a cucumber, both figuratively and literally.

"Remember to stay focused on Alex," he said, coming to a stop at the foot of the bed.

I looked to where my fingers were interlaced with Alex's, and then closed my eyes again. For all Alex and I had been through together, the touch felt unnatural. "I don't get why this is necessary. You were miles away when you dream-bombed Ruby."

"I was already ancient by then. I *knew* stuff."

"*Stuff.* Eloquent. I see the company you've been keeping lately has rubbed off on you." And possibly all over him.

"Will you focus? Remember—only *you* can control yourself. It may be his dream, but you can be active in it. It's a matter of will."

I closed my eyes. "You told me." As I'd suspected, I was supposed to use the same trick I did for flying. Visualize what I wanted to achieve, and believe it was possible. The reason most vampires can't fly is because they can't believe they're able to defy gravity by sheer force of will. I'm generally very selective with what I consider impossible. A certain threesome, for example.

"Cherry? Are you okay?"

"No, I'm not. I'm trying to sleep, and you won't shut up."

He grunted, and I briefly cracked open an eyelid to see him glaring down at me.

"Maybe you shouldn't be here?" I said.

"Not an option. He might attack you again."

"Yeah, 'cause he looks so scary, all unconscious like this."

Constantine frowned. "Perhaps I should try to put you under."

I almost sat up at that. "Like, with vampire mojo? You can actually mind-control vampires? Why didn't you tell me? It would fall into the things-that-concern me category."

"Hush. It has nothing to do with vampirism. I worked with a travelling magician once. He taught me the ways he used to reduce tension and hypnotize select members of his audience."

Pop went my eyelids again. I had to see if he said all that with a straight face.

"Oh, will you sleep, already?" he asked.

"Show me."

"I'd rather drain you again." He ran his tongue over the tip of his elongated fang.

"Whatever."

Neither or us talked after that. I tried hard to focus on Alex, but remembering all the good stuff wasn't so easy this time. The badness was too pronounced and too recent for me to push aside.

I'm ashamed to admit it took a while before it dawned on me that the center of my focus didn't necessarily have to be something positive. I had to zone in on Alex. The specific aspect of him that drew my thoughts was immaterial.

I remembered the way he crowded Constantine in the kitchen. The way he'd grabbed me earlier. How he didn't seem willing to pay heed to my objections, but kept pushing. Touching me.

How he'd been drinking from humans who looked like me.

How he'd almost drained me, after doing nothing to stop Ádísa from blowing him in his dream.

I felt my feet slide. Dead leaves beneath my bare soles.

The smell of rain—

I'm in again.

I'm not standing; I lie sprawled on a heap of leaves. They're slimy with dew, but I can't spare the time to be disgusted.

Two feet away stands Willoughby, arms crossed over his chest, his impeccably white shirt glinting in the moonlight.

"Finally," he says. "I was almost certain you'd manage to fuck this up too." His words are loud as a gunshot in the absolute quiet surrounding me.

I can move. This time I can move. I need to remind myself, before I manage to scramble backward. I look around. It's the same clearing, but in the night it seems dreary. Even malicious. There's still no sound reaching my ears. Not even the squelching of the leaves and dirt under my toes, as I propel my body farther from my maker.

My head hits something hard. A tree. I blink, and Willoughby is closer. Close enough for me to—

I kick out my right leg with all my force.

It doesn't move.

I call on every dredge of inner strength I have. I know this is possible. I did it mere seconds ago. I can move. I can control my actions. I can kick Willoughby on the shin.

No, I can't.

"What did you do?" I try to ask, but the words remain trapped inside me.

Relax. I need to relax. This is just a dream. If I can't control it, I'll wake up.

Willoughby throws back his head and releases an uproarious laugh. "She actually thinks she will somehow survive this."

I don't know who he's talking to.

Wait. I know who he's talking to.

The queen bitch floats toward us, her stride more elegant than her muscled legs ever managed in life or unlife. "Let her hope. It will make her defeat all the more delicious."

Alex materializes next to her, as though out of thin air. His body is first a shimmer. A splotch of light in the dark. The splotch grows and solidifies. She's holding his hand.

I try to look at my hand, the one holding his in the real world, but my fingers aren't in my line of sight, and I can't move my head. I'm trapped here, unable to even close my eyes when Ádísa cups Alex's cheek with her free hand and guides his mouth to hers.

"This time you'll do it," she whispers against his lips.

A fist clenches around my unbeating heart when Alex melts into the kiss.

"This is just a dream," I chant in my head.

Willoughby gives me a scornful look. "How wrong you are."

If it's Alex's dream, how can my maker know my thoughts?

"You won last time," Willoughby says, "but it was sheer luck. Your precious Constantine won't be able to save you this time."

What's everyone's obsession with Constantine? He wasn't saving me when he ripped Ádísa's head off. He was saving himself. She planned on offing both of us. All of us— Alex included. I scowl at Willoughby, hoping my gaze shows exactly what I think of him.

"Oh, you may speak. This will be the last time we hear your annoying voice anyway," he says.

I test my vocal cords by clearing my throat. Sound comes out. Instead of wasting it on my maker, I call for Alex.

Alex, who is still kissing her, his palms curved around the weight of her full breasts.

He doesn't stop kissing her. Doesn't stop squeezing the perfect creaminess I'm seeing way too much of.

"Alex, please," *I whisper. The sight of him responding so eagerly to her advances is breaking me in a way his almost draining me earlier couldn't have done.*

Wake up. I have to wake up, if he won't.

"He can't hear you. Ádísa has him now." *Willoughby says her name as if she's more than his maker. A goddess, perhaps.* "He belongs to her. You can scream his name till you lose your voice again, but this time she's won. Pity you won't be around to see her become her true self again."

For a change, my mind latches onto the important detail. "Where will I be?" *I ask.*

Willoughby raises both arms, palms up. "Everywhere. You'll be scattered by the first gust of wind, once Alex finishes the job."

"The job?"

"Choosing her, and in doing so, killing you."

Fuck, I need to wake up. Now. Wake up and tell Constantine what Willoughby is planning. Alex's subconscious is trying to warn me through his memory of Willoughby, and if his subconscious still cares, I can appeal to the rest of him.

"Alex," I call out again. "Please stop. Please remember who you are. What you know about her. This isn't you."

Only, whoever it is, he's obviously enjoying himself, even as Ádísa rips open his T-shirt and scratches a line from his collar bone to his navel. It's a shallow cut, barely bleeding. Alex hisses in an unnecessary breath and tangles his fingers in her hair, to bring her mouth to his chest. "Lick it," he says, voice gruff with what I recognize as lust.

I've lost him this time.

"She's obviously won. He's with her now. Choice is made. Why does he have to kill me, too?" I try to stall for time, unsure what I'm hoping for. *Divine intervention can't reach me here.*

Why can't I wake the fuck up?

"You will never wake up again, Cherry. God, you've always been so dense." Ádísa nuzzles Alex's stomach, but looks straight at me, the sapphire around her neck lighting her face with an eerie blue glow. "We're not figments of Alex's imagination. His subconscious isn't doing this." She glides a palm down the front of his jeans, and he bucks his hips against it. "I am really me, and it's really Willoughby holding you down, like the powerless little cunt you are."

Turning her face up to meet Alex's gaze, she says, "Let me touch you. Please."

If she's telling the truth, there's no getting out of this. My only advantage over her in the real world is that she's dead, which isn't the case here. There's two of them, ancient and half-past crazy, and only one of me. I can't count on Alex to take my side, even if I don't believe he'll really help them.

I need a weapon.

The only thing I can think of is Ádísa's ego.

"Makes sense," I say, "that even when you control someone's dreams, you need to beg for their affections."

She doesn't take the bait. Her lips are fixed in a smug smile, when Alex pops his fly and pulls his jeans down his hips.

I can't close my eyes, so I settle for rolling them. "Your hold on him only works when you're touching him. I remember you using sex to win Constantine over too, and he ended up dusting you for me."

This time her smile falters, but it doesn't fall from her face. "Constantine fell for your innocent act. The women in your family seem to have the damsel-in-distress bit down to a pat. Alex is smarter than that, though." She closes her hand around Alex's cock, slides it to the base and squeezes, until the head turns an angry purple. "Aren't you, lover?"

Alex moans and begins fucking her fist, one hand pulling on her hair, pushing her head downward. I almost wish she'd take him in her mouth, so I don't have such a clear view of her pleasuring him. What she's doing to him is essentially rape. Even if he's a willing participant, his consent is not informed. He thinks he's dreaming, while according to her, this is actually happening.

"Alex." I make one last effort to concentrate on everything that's passed between us from the moment we hooked up until he started changing. I need to believe he can feel the love I try to broadcast his way, and break her spell.

For a split second, I think I may have succeeded. He inclines his head toward me, and his eyes hold immeasurable sorrow. "Cherry loves me." His voice holds no conviction. He grabs Ádísa's wrist, stops her, but his hips are still thrusting forward. "I can't. I love Cherry," he says, louder this time.

Ádísa frees her hand and stands.

Is she giving up?

No. She pushes at his shoulders, until Alex takes a step back and lets her lower him to the ground. He opens his mouth to talk, but she hushes his protest with a finger across his lips.

"I love Cherry," he says once more.

She smiles. "Not enough, though."

I expect her to straddle him and compound my misery, horror, and disgust, but she passes her palm over his face. "Sleep."

"Didn't you get the memo?" I snark, therefore I am. "He's already asleep. We're in his dream. And if you're done perving all over him, it's time for us to wake up and for you to go back to being nothing but a memory." Is that a quaver in my voice?

I've almost forgotten Willoughby, until he speaks. "You still believe you'll wake from this? That there is an after for you?"

I snort. "There's obviously an after for her, and Constantine twisted her overly made-up head off." Until now, I've more or less been flying by the seat of my pants, going for the what-if scenarios. 'What if Alex's subconscious kind of hates me?' turned into, 'What if psycho bitch and her boy toy are really real?' and to, 'What if I can keep her talking?'

Now I realize that, to see where the latter may lead, I have to focus on the hows.

"How is she here, anyway?" I ask.

Ádísa approaches us. I can see Alex's prone form behind her, his face placid and body limp. "She is eternal." The bitch says.

I laugh. "Not the tune you played when Constantine got rid of you."

"But I'm still here." Her calm grin is disconcerting.

"So you say. Prove it."

"I need prove nothing to you, girl." Her voice turns deeper, older. It bounces off the trees surrounding us, as though they were walls, and reaches my ears in a rumble. "I am who I am. You can only see my aftereffects, and you will—as have those who came before you."

There we go with the riddles again. "Are you being cryptic on purpose," I ask, "or simply unable to carry a normal conversation?"

I don't see her move, but I feel the sting of her slap on my cheek. Tears of anger burn my eyes. I've never felt so vulnerable. Not even last time she tried to kill me. I won't give her the satisfaction of showing it, though. "So it's door number two, then." If I could, I'd toss my hair back.

Ádísa kneels in front of me. Initially I'm irrationally afraid she'll kiss me too. She seems about to, with how close she brings her lips to mine. "Maybe I should fuck one of you. See what all the fuss is about." She scrutinizes my face. "Nah. I think I can live with not knowing." She stands again, and now I'm looking at a pale thigh. Creepy crawlies make their way up my spine, when she says, "I'd rather get rid of you." Alex's subconscious can't possibly be making up the hatred in her tone.

"But why?" My bravado deflates as the certainty she is who she says, and not a faded memory, takes root.

She walks backward, until I can look into her face. "Because I'm done, Cherry. I'm tired of seeking your line up and down the world, vying for the attention of mortals whom I wouldn't spare a second glance. I'm fed up with rejection upon rejection, for the sake of the same women who ultimately spawned you. That's why I had Willoughby turn you."

To my left, Willoughby preens as if she's given him a compliment. 'Cause bleeding an unsuspecting woman dry in the back of a limo, while making out with her, is apparently an accomplishment.

I don't voice my thoughts, because Ádísa is still talking. "As a vampire, you'd be the last of your line, and I could focus my efforts on you. I mean, look at us. How hard could it be to convince someone to leave you *for me?"*

Too hard, as it turned out.

"I guess I could have waited for you to have a loving boyfriend, and then killed you. That way, I could take advantage of his grief, but I tried killing the women before. It never works. The men won't get over them. Constantine didn't, even after you made it clear you didn't want to see him again. It's been what? Six months?"

"Four years plus change—but who's counting?"

"Whatever. You were together for less than it takes me to braid my hair. You should have been nothing to him, yet he killed me for you."

Ah huh. "So you are *dead."*

"Not as dead as you'd want me to be. Tell me, Cherry Stem, what is it about women in your family that makes their men so loyal?"

This is the complete question. Now I finally know what she meant last time we'd met. "Maybe we simply don't fall for men who would go for deranged murderous bitches," I say.

She gives me a strange look, devoid of the anger I expected. "I will never understand the attraction, and I've made my peace with it. I just want it all to end, and I want to return to my rightful place. It is why I planned for Constantine to become your lover. Stealing him back would seal the deal and release me from this limited shell." She looks at her immaculate body with as much disdain as I usually save for my belly rolls.

If she dislikes this *form, how stunning did she originally look? Never mind. I don't want to know. I have enough complexes already.*

"So you wanted to get your Valkyrie cred back, but Constantine threw a wrench in your plans when he wanted to win me back." I can't entirely suppress my smugness.

"Valkyrie? You believe that?" She laughs, the sound too beautiful to be coming from a creature as evil as she is. "Valkyries don't exist. I was so much more. So much stronger. I brought men to their knees, and they begged me to kill them with my love. I was a succubus, favored by Satan himself."

My turn to laugh. "I see death has amplified your delusions of grandeur."

She acts as though she hasn't heard me. "Constantine was one of my greatest disappointments. No matter what I did, his soul was never far from yours. And this is why I'm going to take Alex from you." There's the devious smirk that makes my stomach lurch. I don't believe for a moment she was what she claims to have been, but she's still lethal.

If I'm to save Alex, I have to save myself first. "You have him. Now leave me alone."

She shakes her head. "What I have is a man convinced the woman he loves is in love with another. He may do many interesting, deliciously depraved things with me, but he hasn't chosen me. Not until he kills you."

"But that's—"

"A loophole." Her smile is like a shark's. "The way the condition was worded, he has to kill you for me, because I say so, not because he loves me."

Fuck. Can we get back to trying to wake up?

"It won't make a difference what you do." Willoughby's face appears impossibly close to mine, his pupils taking up most of his irises. "This dream is my playground. What I say goes, and I say Alex will drain you for her. For my maker. She will return and bathe in your blood."

"I thought I'd be drained by then. Best she'll be able to do is snort my powdery remains." My boldness is completely fake. Right now, I don't believe there's a way to survive this dream. Not unless Constantine figures out something's wrong and magically jumps in here with me.

"You can jest all you want, but the result will be the same." Willoughby snaps his fingers, and my limbs shift. Lift. Straighten. My ass glides up the tree trunk I butted my head on, until the entire length of my body presses ramrod straight against that same trunk.

"Alex will drink you to death, proving Ádísa's victory." Willoughby brushes invisible specks of dust off his shoulders. He takes his time unbuttoning his sleeves and rolling them up to his elbows. "Then I will carve out his heart with my fingers and offer it to her. She will be restored, and after I'm done with your friends and family, there won't be anyone left to remember you ever existed."

I try to swallow past the knot in my throat, but find it impossible. Killing me won't be enough for the twisted dynamic duo. They have to obliterate all traces of my passing from this world. "How are you doing this? You're not even Alex's maker, I am. I should have more power over his dreams than you do. Constantine said you can visit the dreams of someone whose blood you've tasted. But to control them?" *It's imperative I understand before I die.*

"I am more than a thousand years old, Cherry. I know more than you ever dreamt of."

"Constantine is older than you," I say.

"But he hasn't spent that time learning. Researching our nature. That's why I knew how to bring her back." *His eyes are burning with fanaticism. He'd lay his life on the line for Ádísa. There's no talking sense into him.* "The only thing I didn't know was that Ruby walks in the sun," he says, "but now our dear Alex has informed me, I am certain your mother will eventually tell me all I need to know, to duplicate Ruby's elixir of life."

"She doesn't know how," I whisper.

"She doesn't know she knows. I can dig into her memories. It'll be painful, of course."

My dead heart constricts in my chest, but I can't let myself believe he can get to my mother. I have to trust Constantine to protect her, as he's done before.

"With you out of the way and the curse broken, Ádísa and I can finally realize our plan," Willoughby says.

Right. The world-domination thing. I'll give you one guess how that went down last time.

If your answer was, 'Like a lead balloon,' congrats, you have more common sense than your run-of-the-mill megalomaniacal vampire.

"Let's take over the world today, Pinky," I mutter under my breath. I look at Ádísa. She's standing over Alex, looking down at him with pure hunger. I'm not sure she'll spare a moment's thought to Willoughby, once she's back to her true nature—whatever that may be—but he won't believe me if I try to warn him.

Constantine will stop them. He will. He has to.

"No, he won't."

I should have realized sooner. The fucker can read my mind.

"It's not that hard. You basically broadcast your thoughts. More to the point, I already told you this dream is mine to play with."

"Then why don't you get on with it? Have Alex kill me, if you think you can." I have no doubt he can, but at this point, death may be easier than listening to these two planning my demise, and I'm not going to beg them for my life.

"Oh, we first had to make sure you'd convince your lover to do what we need," Ádísa says.

Huh?

"He'd never kill you because I asked him to." She fiddles with the end of her braid, the gesture almost innocent. "But if I told him the only way to ensure you stopped wanting Constantine was to drink all your blood, he might."

I narrow my eyes. I can do that much now, even if I can't flex my pinkie.

"Oh, wait," she says. "I've already told him that's the way to your heart. I've made sure to keep him company in his dreams for a while. I've warned him about Constantine's efforts to steal you back. Fed into his jealousy. But he needed to hear it from you. And now you've spent your precious last moments thinking how Constantine could help you. Only Constantine. He'll be the one to save your parents. He'll stop Willoughby and me. Such faith in a man who's betrayed you."

She tuts. "Pity Alex heard those thoughts as clearly as we did. He's heartbroken, the poor dear. He'll do anything in his power not to lose you. Even if it means killing you."

No. I have to wake up.

I have to open my eyes before Alex does. Open my eyes open my eyes open my eyes open my eyes

I opened my eyes to complete darkness.

I was awake. I had to let people know what was happening.

I tried to get off the mattress—why was it wet, anyway?

I wasn't in bed.

Chapter Twenty

I smelled moist earth and dead leaves, and the electricity in the air that usually meant a storm was near. Before I could focus my night sight, I heard a rustling.

"Constantine?" I croaked.

"Guess again." My vision adjusted in time to make out Alex's disdain. The storm was in his eyes, as his fangs popped out, the right one nipping his lower lip enough that a drop of blood welled up to the surface.

"You'll be mine," he said and planted one hand on my mouth, silencing my scream. "Shhh. It's okay. Things will soon be as they should."

I shook my head from side to side as violently as I could, but it didn't stop Alex from grabbing a fistful of my hair, yanking it to one side until my neck hurt, and slicing his fangs into my throat. The memory of him doing the same thing earlier—how being incapacitated and waiting for death had felt—made my panic flare.

This time there was no doubt in my mind he'd finish me off. The long pulls he drew of my blood proved he was determined to.

His body squashed me to the wet ground. We were in the forest. The fucking clearing. How had he brought me here?

I let my own fangs descend and buried them into the flesh of his palm. Surprised, he yanked it away. He only stopped drinking to say, "Scream if you want. Call for Constantine. He's not coming this time. Nobody is." He was set on finishing what he'd started.

I screamed until my voice was hoarse and my throat raw.

I screamed until I no longer had the strength to pull in my lungs the air necessary for another call for help.

Alex kept drinking.

What undid me—what made my gut hurt and revolt at the same time, was the way he stroked my face while he did so. Tenderly. Lovingly. He really believed this was the way to truly be with me.

We were both doomed.

"Alex," I whispered, "I never cheated on you. I never would. Ádísa made you believe I still wanted Constantine, because she needs this. She needs you to kill me."

He pulled back, wiped his mouth on the back of his hand, and looked at me incredulously. "Kill you? I'd never hurt you. I love you." He seemed wounded at the thought. "I'm consuming you. Making you mine."

My fault for not filling him in on the basics of vampirism. I spared a thought to lamenting the loss of VSS. Under the old council, the first thing VSS taught every fledgling was ways we could die, and being drained of blood stood prominent among those.

"You *are* killing me. Once you've drunk the last of my blood, I'll turn to dust." Was it possible to reason with him? Was there still hope? "Ádísa wants you to believe this will make our bond stronger, but she's lying. Why would she come on to you, if she wanted us to be together? She's using you to regain her Valkyrie status." Easier to believe in Valkyries than Succubusses. Succubi. Whatever. "Don't you see?"

Doubt clouded his eyes. "She said you'd try to persuade me not to do it. That Constantine's hold on you is too strong, and you don't want to break it."

I coughed, the strain to keep talking quickly sapping the last dregs of my energy. "She's a liar, Alex. A fucking liar. She wants you to kill me. It's her endgame." Had my eyelashes always been so heavy?

"Hush, baby. You're confused. You just relax, and I'll make it all okay." He touched his lips gently to mine.

"No, you won't," I said in a breath. "She made you attack women who looked like me. She made you doubt my love. And now she's making you kill me. We're all her puppets." With every word, I felt my second life slip away.

He snapped his head back, his expression bouncing from stricken to horrified. "I'm killing you?"

I tried to nod. Speak. Nothing. I hoped he read my blink correctly.

He shook his head, like a horse shaking off a horsefly. "That's— No. I'm not. I'm giving us another chance."

"Says who?" Only his vampire hearing could catch that; my voice was barely audible.

"Ádísa. She said you still love Constantine."

"She lied. Now she wins." My lips were numb. Frozen. Near impossible to move. "I love you," I mouthed, before I could no longer keep my eyes open.

"Cherry? *Wake up.*" He lifted me from the shoulders and pulled me to him. I forced my eyelids open a sliver. His gaze was clear. Ádísa and my asshole of a maker didn't control him in that moment. "This isn't working like she said it would," he yelled.

No shit, Sherlock. I felt like laughing, but it was too much effort.

"I love you too, baby. Fuck. I'm such an idiot. Fuck." Alex scrambled upright, holding me to him. "Blood. You need blood. Then we'll—"

I didn't hear the end of that sentence, because I was harshly thrown back down. I felt rocks digging into my back. Leaves scrunching under my weight. Grass scratching my bare arms.

Dazed, but with adrenaline giving me a second wind, I looked around. Willoughby had tackled Alex to the ground.

He sat on Alex's stomach and pummeled Alex's face with his fists. Alex kept trying to block or return the hits, but Willoughby moved fast as lightning, his eons of experience putting Alex's police training to shame.

Hey, stop that, I thought I said. I made no sound. I made no move. I lay there and watched my maker rain hits on my lover, berating him for being unable to follow through.

"You had one job," Willoughby said. Alex blocked a punch to his temple only to gain himself another in the nose. The crunching sound raised my hackles. "I incapacitated Constantine for you, and even dragged her all the way to the middle of nowhere." My maker closed his fists together and brought them down full-force into Alex's sternum.

He'd kill him, and then he'd have to kill me himself, to keep me from going to the council. There was a twisted sense of vindication in the thought Ádísa wouldn't be getting her loophole salvation after all.

Alex and I would still be dead, but you win some, you lose some.

"You have to stop getting into these damsel-in-distress scenarios." I knew the voice, and I knew the cologne scenting the pale skin of the wrist filling my vision.

Constantine.

"Bite, woman. Take enough to stay awake, while I clean up your mess."

Of all the arrogant, sexist things to say… When I bit into his vein, I made it hurt a little. I took barely half a pint, the whole time watching the pitifully uneven fight unfolding in front of me. Willoughby was too busy turning Alex's head to pulp, to notice the three of us were no longer alone in the clearing.

I didn't bother to lick the wound closed. "Go," I said. "I'll be okay, as long as you keep him away from me."

Constantine didn't have to be told twice. He literally flew into Willoughby's body, lifting him in the air and slamming him down on a log. It was the one Alex had sat on, when he'd sleepwalked to this clearing. I hoped Constantine broke the asshole's spine.

Willoughby scissored his legs in the air, kicked, and twisted his body, torque setting him upright, as Constantine reached for his head. Spine intact, then. Bummer. Judging from the murder in Constantine's eyes, that wouldn't remain the case for long.

Alex tried to sit up, but before he could lift his body off the ground, Willoughby avoided a high kick by Constantine, produced a stake from his jacket pocket, and slammed it into Alex's upper chest.

"Alex. *No.*" This time my voice was loud. My throat still hurt, but not as much as my heart did. It took an eternity for me to realize Alex hadn't dusted. Willoughby hadn't found his heart. He'd merely—*merely*—staked him to the ground.

Constantine tried to repeat his attack through the air, but this time Willoughby was prepared. He rolled to his back and kicked both legs into Constantine's stomach. It was like watching a superhero movie, with bodies and fists taking off and descending like rockets, kicks connecting with the force of minivans, and nobody making enough headway to be deemed the winner.

I absentmindedly noticed the real forest came with real forest sounds. A squirrel scurried up the tree to my right and scared a bird into flight.

"Ádísa wanted to take care of you herself, but she'll have to settle for my avenging her death." Willoughby managed to smash a knee into Constantine's lower back, making him jackknife backward.

"She will not have a say in the matter, because she is not coming back. Ever." Doing a close resemblance of a backflip, Constantine grabbed Willoughby's lapels—seriously, who wore a button-down to a fight in the woods?—and sent them both hurtling into the thick foliage surrounding us.

"Oh, she is." Willoughby knocked him backward, his entire bodyweight behind the blow. "Even if I have to slice your whore's throat and let the blood drip into Alex's mouth." He feinted to the left, and when Constantine mirrored him, dove toward me.

"*No.*" Constantine's roar was deafening. Willoughby was almost upon me, when Constantine wrapped both arms around his waist and pulled him away.

My maker used the momentum to roll around and pin Constantine to the ground beneath him. They were inches from me, and I was powerless to stop Willoughby from locking Constantine's head in a vice-like grip.

"You'll dust for what you did to Ádísa," Willoughby said. His eyes held the same murderous glint they had in the dream, as he began twisting Constantine's head around.

"*Cherry.*"

I glanced up to see Alex grasp the stake buried in his chest. It's funny what the mind focuses on in times of grave danger. I saw his knuckles turn white with the effort it took to drag the piece of wood out of his flesh. As soon as it cleared the wound, he tossed it to me in a high arch, and his head fell back, his last reserves of energy depleted.

I raised my hand and prayed his aim would be true. There would be no second chance to do this.

The moment the rough, unpolished piece of wood touched my palm, I closed my fingers around it. With strength and precision I didn't know I still possessed, I swung and slammed it into Willoughby's back.

I felt flesh give way under the pointy tip, muscle shred, and bone shift.

And I felt his black, shriveled heart tear.

I felt it. Inside my own chest. I'd died and come back before, but had never experienced the violent ripping sensation I did now. Or the sad, *sad* hollowness that unfolded in my chest. Was that how it felt when someone's maker died? If I hurt like someone stomped on my stomach and squeezed my throat at the same time, when I'd barely known and completely hated my maker, how had Constantine felt when he'd ripped his own maker's head off? She'd been his companion. His lover. His love.

A puff of dust exploded all over Constantine and me, getting into our eyes and mouths, and dispersing the blackness inside me, until it was little more than a dull ache. I spat out the foul, bitter taste, but could feel a ferocious grin threatening to split my face in half.

We'd done it. We'd fucking done it. The bastard who'd ended both my and Alex's lives was no longer.

Exhilaration faded away, giving its place to exhaustion. I wished I could pass out, so one of the men would carry me home, but A) I'm a vampire, and we don't pass out when we're tired, and B) no way was I giving Constantine fodder for more damsel-in-distress jokes.

Alex crawled to me, and Constantine sat back and let him gather me in his arms. My ex's gaze was watchful, and when Alex tried to offer me blood, Constantine stopped him with a gentle shake of his head. "You look as if you spent the night in a meat grinder, and you've been staked. Let me."

I looked up at Alex's face. It was beginning to heal, but it was still bloody and raw, his nose at an odd angle. He glanced at me, then Constantine, and I was relieved to see no hint of speculation or distrust in his eyes. "I've taken a lot of her blood," he said. "I have enough to spare. You've already fed her."

"Twice," Constantine said, "but I don't need as much as you do to sustain me."

"Yeah, yeah, you're ancient." My joke fell flat. I let them maneuver me into Constantine's lap.

"Do you want me to fix your nose for you?" he asked Alex.

"Nah, I got it." Alex closed his fist over the bridge of his nose and gave it one hard yank, twisting his wrist. "Fuck."

I was pondering whether to ask how much pain he was in, or tell him it served him right, when I felt Constantine's tongue on my neck. I shivered at the cool, wet stroke. "What..?" My voice came out way too breathy, for someone who'd been through Hell and back.

"Just taking care of your wounds." His voice was emotionless, but his grip on my arm quivered. The intimate gesture had rattled him.

It had rattled me too. "How did you find me?" I asked. "Us."

"I'll always find you," Constantine replied.

His words soothed and unsettled me at the same time, but before I could ask more, I felt a whisper close behind. It was the same sensation I'd had in Alex's dream—the familiar-yet-not presence. I snapped my head around, almost head-butting Constantine. Nobody was there. "Did you feel that?"

Constantine gave me a smile too wide to be honest. "I'm sure I don't know what you mean."

Before I could explain or demand a straightforward answer, Alex kneeled by my side and took my hand. "I'm so sorry, Cherry. I'm willing to spend eternity making this up to you."

Constantine cleared his throat. "Let us start by getting her back to her feet. Then you two can patch things up, while I take the time to sunbathe, like it is going out of fashion."

I half chuckled, half choked at his choice of phrasing.

"You want my wrist again?" he asked.

The way I sat, my face so close to his, drinking from his throat would have been infinitely easier. Natural.

Dangerous.

"Yeah," I said.

I opened his vein, careful not to spill a drop or cause any unnecessary pain. I drank and sealed the wound. I tried to keep the process clinical and remain detached from the feelings and memories drinking from him a third time in a row brought to the surface. It wasn't easy, with our bodies pressed together.

"Ready," I said and used Constantine's shoulder as a prop to get myself upright.

Alex tried to drape one of my arms over his shoulders, but I shied away from his touch. It wasn't a voluntary reaction. I've said before that the body has a memory of its own, and sometimes it overcomes reason. I knew Alex hurt for hurting me, but my body couldn't take his proximity.

His face was healing, but I was thankful his still swollen eyes hid his feelings when he gave me a brisk nod and walked ahead to lead the way out of the woods.

Constantine helped me along the path. "You'll be okay," he said. "Both of you."

"I know." I told myself it was exhaustion that made me cling to him, not the need for reassurance. "Thank you," I whispered.

He looked away, but not before I saw the thin line of his usually luscious mouth. "I would have come sooner, but I was detained."

"Detained?" I tripped over a fallen branch.

He held me up, his arm wrapping tighter around my waist. "Willoughby came by your parents' house. He must have compelled one of them to let him in."

I halted and turned him to face me. "My parents? Are they—?"

"They're fine. They were sleeping when I left. Both breathing; I made sure. Willoughby probably didn't want to kill them until he got everything he needed."

I wouldn't think of the lengths he might go to make my mom tell him the recipe for the potion. I would focus on my relief he hadn't harmed them.

"I didn't realize he was there until he burst in the basement bedroom and ordered Alex to take you to the forest. We fought, and he staked me to the wall." Constantine clacked his tongue. "Apparently Ádísa would love that."

"She totally would." A short laugh burst out of my lips.

He chuckled and looked somewhere behind me. "You realize she is to blame for everything. Alex was her puppet."

My eyes stung. I rubbed my face with both hands and wasn't surprised to see blood and dirt on my palms when I was done. "I know." I wasn't happy she could make him her puppet, though.

"Good." He tucked me to his side, and we caught up with Alex, who'd almost reached the end of the tree line.

Chapter Twenty-one

We made it home with the gray light of dawn and went straight to the basement. It wouldn't do to freak out my parents with our blooded and bruised appearance.

"You hit the shower first," I told Alex.

He complied without a word, and a fist gripped my insides, threatening to rip me apart. I should say something soothing to him, but I didn't want to.

Constantine watched Alex shuffle his feet to the small bathroom. I stepped aside to give Alex wide berth, and Constantine pinned me with his gaze.

"Resentment is a nasty thing. Sneaky," he said, when the door was safely closed between us and Alex. "It burrows inside you and makes a nest. It festers there and rots your soul."

"Same goes for jealousy," I said. "At least there's a good enough reason for my feelings."

He crossed the room to me. His six-foot-something towered over my five-foot-four, but I didn't feel threatened, even when he leaned close and trapped me between his body and the wall.

He brought his lips to my ear. "And you're saying Alex had no reason to be jealous?"

I heard water running behind me. Alex showered a few feet from us.

Constantine feathered his lips over the shell of my ear. He smelled of his cologne and blood and moist earth. I closed my eyes and let my head drop back. I owed it to him to be honest, but I didn't know how.

In the end, I said, "I never gave him reason to." It would have to suffice.

Constantine inhaled deeply in my hair, and then touched his forehead to mine. "That I don't think you should condemn him for things beyond his control doesn't mean I have given up on you," he whispered.

His lips were a hair's breadth from mine. He'd kiss me. Did I want him to?

He stepped back, and relief and disappointment warred for room inside me.

He trained his gaze to the floor. "We cannot control what we feel. What we want. Fortunately, in most cases we can control what we do about it. In the end, Alex chose you."

I nodded, quietly.

"You should shower after he's done," Constantine said. "I'll use the upstairs bathroom." He left me no time to reply.

I waited for Alex to come out, holding a pair of sweatpants and a Tee for each of us away from my body, so I didn't stain them. He came out, wrapped in a towel. We avoided each other's gaze, as I handed him his clothes.

I took the fastest shower in history. I didn't want to smell Alex's blood and body gel any longer than I had to. It jumbled up my brain, sending warm and fuzzy feelings to my belly and jolts of terror through my core.

I pulled on my pants and shirt, and fled the bathroom.

Alex gathered our torn and blooded clothes into a pile, and we shoved them into the big garbage bag Constantine brought downstairs with his own tattered clothing. I braided my wet hair hurriedly, and tried to apply some makeup on my neck but gave up. There was no reason to put effort into hiding the bruises. They'd fade and disappear all together after a good feeding.

I took in Alex and Constantine's faces. Alex's cheeks had deep gashes, and the bones seemed broken. His nose was swollen, and angry purple blotches circled his eyes.

Constantine only had a few cuts on his forehead, but the knuckles of his left hand looked like raw hamburger.

By comparison, the two bite marks on my neck, were nothing.

A hole in the wall of the bedroom marked the spot where Willoughby had skewered Constantine to the wall. Despite all his scheming, that was all the lasting damage he'd managed to do today, and it would be fixed with some plaster and paint.

I felt hysterical laughter bubble up my throat and clenched my teeth together. That wasn't all of it. Alex, Constantine, and I were still here, my parents were still alive, Ádísa was still dust, but something else had been irreparably dented.

My relationship with Alex.

****

We found Mom in the kitchen, preparing breakfast.

"My God, what happened to you?" Her gaze zoomed in on Alex, then took in Constantine and me.

"We got Willoughby," I said.

Mom wiped her hands on her apron, and rushed to hug me so fiercely I thought my bones creaked. "Are you okay?" she asked.

"We're fine. Well, not fine, but nothing a little blood won't fix."

"You should see the other guy." Alex's chuckle turned into a groan. "I can't even laugh."

He'd tried to kill me. Twice. Still, he was as much a victim as I was. I patted his shoulder, and he rubbed his cheek on my knuckles. Maybe my body could forgive, if it couldn't forget.

"Sit. I'll get you blood and some tea," Mom said.

"Don't bother with tea for me. I'm good with blood too," Alex replied.

Mom gave him a questioning look, but got two bags of blood from the freezer and popped them into the microwave. She returned her attention to the skillet in time to salvage five strips of crispy bacon.

"I decided to expand my diet," Alex said. He waited for me to sit first, and then took the seat across from me, leaving Constantine to sit next to me.

"Willoughby is no longer a threat," Constantine said.

"Not thanks to me," Alex muttered.

I'm not sure Mom heard, but she kept nodding as she poured the first large spoonful of pancake batter in the griddle, without cleaning the bacon grease. My mouth watered.

Dad joined us for breakfast, and between us, Alex, Constantine, and I told them what had happened during the night. Alex had the most trouble with it, but his description of the systematic brainwashing Ádísa had done in his dreams was honest.

I cut in before he told them of the first time he almost drained me. "Willoughby and Ádísa made him take me to the woods, but he shook off their control and helped keep Willoughby busy until Constantine came." The more time passed since our fight with Willoughby, the more I thought Alex and I might work things out. If my parents knew the disturbing details, there would be another hurdle for us to overcome, and we already had enough of those.

I reached across the table for Alex's hand, but he fisted it before I could clasp it. He frowned and opened his mouth, but closed it again without speaking.

"And where is she now? Willoughby is dust. Does she have other progeny that could come after you?" Dad asked.

I froze for the second it took Constantine to shake his head. "No. If there was another *childe* of hers out there, we'd know by now. Even if she's not entirely gone, she is no longer a threat. She's suspended somewhere, inert without Willoughby to bring her in touch with the living and undead. There is no way left for her to return to life."

Phew.

"So what now?" Mom studied my face. "Do you have to go?"

I looked at Constantine. "Do we?"

"You can stay for as long as you want. You slew Willoughby, and once I return to L. A. and inform the council, you'll be one of the cool kids." His grin was full of mischief.

"I've always been one of the cool kids. Your stupid council just didn't know it." I held out my plate, and my mother served me a neat stack of pancakes.

"*Our* stupid council now."

So I was going to become a member of the ruling body. Cool. There were some things that needed changing. Especially the stupid rule forcing fledglings to disappear from their families.

Alex was silent until then. Now he asked, "What about me? Am I still the secret bastard of the vampire clan?"

His words lacked bite, and Constantine didn't react to the snark. "I think between Cherry and me, we can convince the others of your value, as well as of the need to allow your continued employment. One of our own in the Los Angeles police force should be handy."

I expected Alex to be happy at that, but he seemed pensive, eyebrows drawn low and nostrils flared.

"So you're staying?" Dad asked.

"I guess so." I smiled. Some tender loving care from my parents would go a long way toward healing us all.

At least, I believed so.

For the next two days, we all stayed with my parents, who coddled us and plied us with packaged blood and Ruby's potion.

After the first couple of feedings, our bodies were fully recovered. Even the holes in Alex's shoulder and Constantine stomach, where Willoughby had run them through with stakes, were completely healed. And Alex now fed solely on bagged blood, which other than a great step toward his full acceptance of his vampire existence was a relief to me. Although at times I missed his more gentle bites, I wasn't sure I could bring myself to feed him.

I did enough soul searching at night, when he slept on the floor by the bed we used to share, to know I still loved him and wanted to make our relationship work. I wasn't sure, though, how long it would be before I could enjoy his touch again. Or even endure it.

I wasn't the only one feeling uneasy. Alex walked on egg-shells around me, treating me as if I were made of porcelain, and Constantine made himself scarce while I was awake.

Their behavior drove me up the walls and kept me from fully enjoying what should be a relaxed time. I tried to mend our relationship, but seemed to be doing something wrong.

The nicer I was to Alex, the more distant he became. We didn't have a single exchange during which he looked me in the eye. His gaze was usually drawn to the floor or ceiling, and he avoided talking about what happ— *No.* About what Willoughby did to us.

I was fed up with his behavior before too long. Yes, we weren't at a good place, but if he wanted to ever make things right, we needed to talk about what happened, not dance around it.

I was still not used to sleeping at night. After fighting to doze off for what seemed like hours, I sat up with a huff. "Alex, about Ádísa…"

He sat on the floor by the bed, not even pretending to try to sleep. "No." He shook his head. "It's too soon. You need to recover first, and—"

"*We* will never recover, if we don't deal with what happened. Alex, I want to be with you. Look at me."

He swung his arm to the side, slammed his fist on the wall, and grimaced when I winced. "I'd say I'd never hurt you, but we'd both know it's a lie," he said.

I got up and approached him slowly, as I would a wounded animal. "I don't believe you'll hurt me again. I know what happened wasn't your fault."

"Wasn't it? She came to me, yes, and I'll even accept she had some psychic influence on me, but she'd have achieved nothing if I wasn't jealous of Constantine."

"Cons—"

"I know you say you and he are in the past, and I believe you believe it, but he loves you, Cherry, and he's a better man than me. Not that it's hard these days."

"It's not a contest. I chose *you*."

"But would you choose me again?" He didn't give me time to answer. "Should you? Ádísa persuaded me with lies and compulsion, and Willoughby urged me on, but I knew I was hurting you. Even if I didn't believe I'd *kill* you, I was still trying to force you to choose me. *Force* you, Cherry."

"I want to be with you." I kept saying that, but after what had transpired between us, I mostly wanted to be by myself for a few days. "My mom said I could stay another week or so. More like, she said she'd hunt me down if I didn't. You and Constantine go home, clear the air between you, and when I get back, we'll start over. I know we're both hurting, but I don't blame you." Not consciously, at least.

"Why didn't she haunt Constantine's dreams?"

"What?" I needed a moment to catch up to what he meant.

"Ádísa could have haunted Constantine's dreams. Why didn't she?"

I thought about it. "Willoughby hadn't drunk his blood."

"But she had, and Willoughby had hers. Cee—Constantine told me that would have worked too. But she didn't go to Constantine, because she knew he would never turn against you."

"He's older, Alex. He'd know she was lying."

"Maybe he's stronger. Maybe he loves you more. Either way, he wouldn't have failed you like I did."

I didn't know what to say, to counteract his argument. Especially without hurting his already wounded ego more. Constantine was stronger, but that was only because of his age.

As for the other thing— "The reason doesn't matter," I said. "Maybe she didn't want to risk it, since he killed her. You know what? You should stay too. Constantine can go, so the vampettes don't take their withdrawal out on Sheena and Wesley, and you'll stay. We'll start over. Maybe date a little. Do things the right way this time." We'd slept together and fallen in love before getting to fully know each other. A new beginning might fix everything.

Alex shook his head. "Dating won't fix this, Cherry. I'm sorry. I can't. I have to go."

"Back to the mansion?" I knew that wasn't what he'd said, but I needed to hope things would get back to how they were.

"Cherry."

His hushed utterance of my name did it. It broke the dam. So far, I had found an excuse for him, every step of the way. He'd been thrown into my world unprepared. His turning had been without his consent. He was forced to leave his apartment and cohabitate with my ex, among several other people living at the mansion. He was used by an ancient Valkyrie—or whatever the fuck she used to be—and her lackey.

But now *he* wanted to leave me, and he didn't even have the decency to yell and have a proper fight about it.

I'd fix that.

"What? Am I making this hard for you? What happened to your promise to make it up to me? You hurt me. Repeatedly. And you think the way to atone for it is to run away? Excuse me for not liking that solution one fucking bit." I'd raised my voice and wasn't surprised to hear a knock on the door.

"Not now," I said.

"Yes, now." Constantine made his way in, as if he owned the room. He had a knack for that.

"We're trying to have a conversation here," I said.

Alex hung his head. "I've already spoken to Constantine about it. He agrees it's for the best."

Just when I thought he couldn't piss me off more. He went to Constantine before he talked to me? And Constantine had—what? Given permission to Alex to dump me? "Does he, now?" I glared at Constantine. "I bet he's only thinking of what's best for our relationship. Or maybe you're being played by yet another ancient vampire."

"I resent that implication." Constantine's lips didn't even move. They were frozen in the most uncomfortable smile I've ever seen him sport. "I am actually trying to salvage your relationship."

"By driving us apart. Makes sense." It had nothing to do with helping us and everything to do with his feelings for me. There was no reason bringing said feelings up in front of Alex, though, when I was trying to convince him there was nothing between Constantine and me.

"I'd already made up my mind when I went to him," Alex said. He stood and took an uncertain step toward me. He dusted the seat of his jeans. He was always fully dressed around me now. "The night Constantine killed Ádísa, she said Los Angeles wasn't the only city they'd been hunting in. With the council's sanction, I'm going to look for other fledglings she and Willoughby were hiding from us."

"The council knows about you?" After all we'd done to hide his change from them? I was dumbfounded.

"You and I do. We're both members now," Constantine said with a shrug. "You and I witnessed Willoughby turn Alex three days ago, before he tried to come after you again, and you took him out."

He'd said this would happen, but I didn't know how to react. What did it mean? What would be my responsibilities? I opted for my usual way of dealing with overwhelming situations—humor. "Do I get a crown?" I asked. "'Cause I really want a crown."

Constantine gave me a look fraught with disapproval, but his eyes were smiling.

"Well, I don't sanction Alex's leaving. He has to stay. We have to work things out."

"I need to go, Cherry. These fledglings need to be brought in and shown they can be good, despite Ádísa's doctrine. If I help them, I help me. I'll learn control as I teach them. I won't trust myself with you unless I know nothing can get to me. That I'm more than my new nature. We can't work anything out until I've found myself again. You and I keep saying I wasn't myself lately, but who was I? Who am I really, now that everything I've known is different?"

Sadness funneled into hurt, and then into anger. "And you're just now figuring out you've changed? You've been a vampire for months."

"Yes, and I pretended everything was the same, but it's not. To be good enough for you—to be the best I can be—I must first figure out a way to be me. This new me. Undead guy on a liquid diet."

"You can be you with me," I said quietly. I'd lost my oomph. Alex was determined, and I wouldn't stoop to begging.

Constantine reached for the door handle. "I will let the two of you hash it out."

"Don't bother," I said. "We're done." I turned to Alex. "Go, but I'm not going to wait for you."

"I wouldn't expect you to, but I *will* return, and I *will* try to win you back." To Constantine, he said, "You hear that? Take care of her, make whatever move you're going to while I'm gone, but I'll fight for her when I'm myself again."

Constantine shrugged. "When Cherry comes back to me, it will not be because I won by default—because I was the one to stay behind. She will come because she burns for me."

I expected a punch to fly his way. Alex gave him a tired smile instead. "You're a weird fuck, Cee, but I can see what she likes about you."

I shook my head in disbelief. I was *there*, while they talked about me like I was a prize to be won. "You're both weird fucks, and I don't like either of you very much right now." Though the discussion turned me on.

"You, pack your bags," I told Alex. "Go, do your thing, and we'll talk when you're back." Something dawned on me. "As a council member, I order you to check in with me when you get to each new city. I want to know where you are at least once a week. Got it?"

"Will do."

"And you"—I poked Constantine in the chest—"better get back home. Your little girlfriends are driving Sheena crazy." I left the room, unwilling to watch Alex get ready to leave. Leave me. "I'm staying with my folks for a couple weeks. I need the time off," I called over my shoulder, already halfway up the stairs.

I didn't see Alex off. Mom said Constantine would drive him to the mansion, to get a bigger suitcase and more clothes, and then take him to the airport. Constantine didn't come see me before he left either. He asked my folks to let me know my room at the mansion would be waiting for me.

Epilogue

I'll go, sooner or later, but it's been ten days, and I still hate the idea of leaving. Having breakfast with my parents in the morning, in a house devoid of vampires, drama, and politics, feels good. Normal.

I've missed normal.

Mom makes tea, and after Dad goes to work, we prepare lunch and fill each other in on the last six years.

I do most of the talking.

I've told her everything—about my short-lived career in porn, about my turning, about what Constantine meant to me and what he still means to me. About Alex. This time I even told her about the change in his behavior toward me and why he left.

I think she's Team Constantine, but first and foremost, she's Team Cherry, and that's what matters.

She even calls me that now, having accepted everything that's changed about me.

My dad knows less, but enough to realize I'm no longer the little girl who left home to make it as a model in the city. I'm still *his* little girl, though. He makes sure to bring me a cupcake every evening, and I'm finally glad for my vampire metabolism, after years of whining about being unable to change my body.

Alex called tonight. He's been in San Francisco since he left. Nothing definitive has come up, but he believes he's on the trail of at least one member of Ádísa and Willoughby's army of undead hotties.

It was the second time he called—the first was to say he landed safely. We didn't speak about us this time either.

I've come to realize there really can't be an *us* right now. I hate to say it, but he made the right choice in leaving. Distance has to soothe the hurt that's there. Soften its edges. When we can look at each other without seeing the past, maybe we can start building again, if there's enough foundation left. He seems to be on the right track to finding himself.

I turned in soon after we hung up. The downside to living with my parents is that I'm worn out well before midnight, and tonight was no exception. The moment my head hit the pillow, I was out like a light.

I'm lying on a sunbed, a strawberry daiquiri in one hand, a romance novel in the other. The warmth of the sun caresses my skin, and a light breeze ruffles my hair from time to time. The only sound disrupting my sunbathing is the gentle, languid sloshing of the sea against the shore.

I've had this dream before. I know the book is blank, but the frozen daiquiri tastes like heaven, the sweetness and tartness of fresh strawberry elevated by the kick of alcohol.

I sense a presence that wasn't here last time, though. I look around, and here's Constantine, strolling along the beach toward me.

He stands over me, in a pair of scruffy jeans he'd never wear if I were awake. No shirt. No shoes. The sand gleams golden between his toes, but it's the pale perfection of his broad chest that draws my gaze. "I miss you," he says. "When are you coming home?"

He feels so real, I know I'm not dreaming of him. He's sharing my dream—or is he usurping it?

I put my drink aside, lower the book to my lap, and push my sunglasses atop my head. "I thought this was supposed to be me-time," I say squinting up.

"You can have you-time at the mansion." He shades his eyes with his palm, and a cloud covers the bright sun, shedding a grey tint over my surroundings.

"Are you controlling my dream? That's not playing fair." I'm not upset, just curious. "You said you didn't know how."

"I'm only doing what I have always done," he says. "Watching out for you."

"Pretty stalkery of you." Part of me wonders at my calm acceptance. Then again, not everything has to make sense in dreams. *"Now if you don't mind, I have several months of tanning to make up for."*

"This is a dream."

"Exactly. Only place I can tan. So unless you're here to put lotion on my back, or have something else to fess up to..." I give him a little finger wave.

I expect him to make some remark about the lotion, but his expression closes, becomes more guarded. He crosses his arms and rests his chin on his chest. *"I promised to never again keep something significant from you, and something came up that I believe falls into that category."*

"Next time use the phone." I reach for my book again, but he drops to his knees and traps my hand between both of his.

"Ruby visited my dream," he says. *"She heard about Willoughby."*

That stings. *"She could have called me. I know you two go back a long time, but I'm her granddaughter. You'd think that'd count for someth—"*

"Cherry, she says you could become human again."

"What?" My whining is forgotten in an instant. Hope blossoms in my heart, but I stomp on it before it takes root. There's no turning back from being undead. If there was, I'd have at least heard rumors about it. *"That's not possible."* Is it?

He snaps his head to one side, then the other. "Shit. I must wake up. Tell nobody of this and don't call me. We can't talk about it over the phone. Just come home."

I nod, and he's gone.

I need to wake up.

Now.

The End

Want more?

Cherry Pie - Chapter One

I open myself to the scenery around me, until the stitches holding it together start glowing a pure white. The sunglasses holding my hair back from my face are useless against this light, but I don't want to dim it, anyway. I need to take it in.

The sight is beautiful in its eeriness.

I focus on a single point along the seam between golden sand and blue morning sky. About where the overhead light switch should be. It doesn't give, but it will. I've been practicing since I was trapped in Alex's dream.

I use my finger to draw a bright-red thread over it. I tug, and my strawberry daiquiri fades to transparency before it's gone completely. The book on my lap follows it to oblivion. The wind has dropped, and the waves no longer lap at the shore. They're frozen in place until I pull again, and then they melt into the sky that in turn gives its place to the white of my bedroom walls.

I close my eyes and smile when the beach chair beneath me yields into something softer. Fluffier. I open my eyes again and—

I blinked away my much-needed sleep. Did Constantine have to drop into my dream tonight of all nights? His timing sucked.

Speaking of timing, I should start keeping track of how long it took to enter and exit a dream. I practiced every chance I got and was improving—another reason I was so tired; I needed to let my mind switch off once in a while—but I wanted tangible results.

Maybe I'd ignore my ex's new bout of drama and sink back into my dream.

Sure.

I'd forget he said I could be human again, so I could catch some shut eye. 'Cause I was cool like that.

Not.

I kicked the sheets off and stood. My inner clock told me the sun was still down for the count, which meant so were my parents. I didn't want to sneak out of their home without saying *goodbye*, but if what Constantine said was true, I couldn't wait to get more details out of him.

I pulled on my jeans and sneakers, and wore my hoodie over Alex's T-shirt I'd been using as a pajama top. His scent was barely there, after ten days. I didn't know where we stood, other than that we weren't a *we*, but I liked feeling close to him at night. And it was a comfy shirt.

I scribbled a quick note for my parents on a Post-it and pressed it to the fridge door with the heel of my hand.

Constantine needs me at the mansion. I'll be back tomorrow, for my stuff and a proper farewell.
And I'll need pancakes. Lots of them.

Love you both,
Cherry

It was a three-and-a-half-hour drive back to L.A. without traffic, but traffic didn't apply to me. I was flying there. I pulled my hair into a tight bun, to minimize damage, and took off.

The crisp night air felt refreshing on my skin and called up memories of the warmth of the dream. The heat had been at its strongest when Constantine was there.

And when wasn't that the case?

As trees and heels gave way to wide open road beneath me, my mind flew forward, to the mansion and the man waiting there.

Constantine hadn't reached out before tonight, respecting my need to spend time with my family. I appreciated that, but until I dreamed of him, topless beside me, I hadn't realized I'd missed him. It was weird. We broke up years ago, but the last few months he'd been a constant in my life and I liked having him around.

Another thing to sort out if I wanted a future with Alex.

Which I did.

With the exception of his dark period, during which my maker and Constantine's messed with Alex's head and turned him into a psycho intent on draining me, Alex was the yang to Constantine's yin. He was open with his feelings, unafraid of commitment, and with a moral compass so strong, you could count on him to always draw a clear line between right and wrong.

Constantine was all about gray areas and fuzzy limits.

And I was confused.

Not about which of them to choose. Constantine was history—though who knows what would have happened between us if Ádísa hadn't planned and executed our breakup?

Not what I should be considering.

The hazy scenery beneath me began gaining shape. I cut into the smog, thankful I didn't have to breathe. I began my decent, careful to keep away from the lights. Not easy in downtown L.A. but doable around Constantine's mansion.

My feet met solid ground at the same time, and I brought my body to a perfect halt. Can I get a *yay* for bending the laws of physics?

I lowered my hood and let my hair loose. It felt stiff, and I bet it looked it, but this wasn't a social call.

Constantine said I could become human again.

How?

And why wasn't I ringing his doorbell and asking him?

I pressed the button by the wrought-iron gate and smiled at the closed circuit camera, waiting for Wesley, Constantine's ancient human butler, to buzz me in.

"Come to the parlor. We'll watch the sunrise." Constantine's voice came from behind me.

I spun on my heel. Nothing. The acoustics in this place were wonky.

The latch clicked, and the gate slid open. "I'm not here for the sunrise," I muttered under my breath, though I couldn't wait to see it. Couldn't get enough sun since my grandmother's potion made it possible for me to walk in daylight again. If only I could tan.

I followed the path to the front door and let myself in. Wesley poked his head out of the kitchen, and a smile brightened his lined face. "You've been missed," he said. "Coffee?"

"I missed you too." I returned the smile. "And yes, please." No need to tell him how I took it; he'd made me coffee more times than I could count, both when I dated Constantine and in the months Alex and I stayed here.

I padded softly on the plush carpet, as I trailed through the ground floor, praying I met nobody else before I talked to Constantine. I'd love to catch up with Sheena, and the little masochist in me missed the three fledglings Constantine sort of adopted on the day he decapitated Ádísa, but I could do without diversions until I had answers to my questions.

From past experience, odds were Constantine would be less than fully dressed, so I wasn't surprised to see him in nothing but a pair of silk pajama bottoms. I crossed the threshold to the spacious room at the exact same moment the rising sun appeared through the wall-to-wall window panes. The rays that a couple weeks ago would have reduced Constantine to ashes now set his pale skin ablaze with red, orange, and purple hues. The muscles in his wide sternum stood out in stark relief, and his blue eyes sparkled.

He was magnificent.

I didn't try to hide my ogling. He expected it. It wouldn't surprise me if he'd timed my entrance specifically for this.

I blinked, and whatever thrall he held over me evaporated. He was still stunning, but now I could focus on things beyond that, like—"You said I could become human again?"

"I did."

I was looking right at him, but I didn't see his lips move.

He nodded, his lips never parting. "Finally, she catches on. I've been dropping hints for a while."

"How are you doing this? Are you messing with my mind?"

He held my gaze. "I've broken my promise," he said. His serious tone was a far cry from the seductive purr he usually opted for when shirtless. "I've kept something important from you."

Ah. "How long have you known I could be turned back?" I glared. Would he never learn? Omissions and lies always came back to bite him in the ass. And I wouldn't think of that thing's perfect curve.

"No, not that. I shared as soon as Ruby told me about it. There's something else." His mouth formed a hard line, but the words kept coming. *"When two vampires who've killed their own makers exchange blood, they get a sort of telepathy."*

Shock and surprise sort-circuited my brain.

"I killed Ádísa, and you killed Willoughby," he said. In my head. *"And then—"*

"You cleaned my wounds and fed me your blood. Three times." In fact, he'd insisted on giving me *his* blood when Alex tried to feed me.

"Yes. And you don't have to speak aloud. I can hear your thoughts."

This was too fucking much. "You do that, and I promise to hurt you so bad, you'll taste it for eternity. My thoughts are mine. No trespassing. Got it?" I refused to use my inside voice.

"Cherry, I would never disrespect you this way. You have to believe me."

"Do I?" I was tired of believing him. Of trusting him. More tired of reminding myself not to. "Don't tell me you only found out about this now, too."

"No." He said this aloud. "I've known for a while, and after Alex… After you were hurt the first time, I couldn't overlook the opportunity."

"To bind me to you?" I asked. The arrogance was strong with this one.

He frowned. "To never let you get hurt again. Wherever you are, whatever happens, you'll be able to reach me at the speed of thought. Think about this, Cherry." His eyes pleaded with me to forgive him, and I found myself wanting to.

"You should have let me choose for myself," I said.

"You were drained. There was no time to discuss it."

"You could have come to me later."

"I didn't think that far ahead." He stood, but I knew all his tricks by now. He used his body as a distraction.

It wouldn't work this time.

"Oh, but you did," I said. "You jumped at the chance to have an in with me, and you knew it when you were telling Alex you wouldn't be my default choice. Games. It's all about games with you."

"There was nothing game-like about seeing you bled out in your parents' basement, with your crazed lover still inside you, and knowing I could have prevented that. You'd be dead now if I hadn't acted."

I arched an eyebrow. "Alex might have stopped." I didn't believe it.

"We both know he wouldn't have, but I'm not talking about then. How do you think I found you in that clearing?"

I remember wondering about that. "But you hadn't had my blood then. You only licked my wounds clean after."

He raked his fingers through his long blond hair. "When I gave you my blood the first time, I held you. Your blood was all over me, driving me insane. I knew the effects wouldn't last if I only tasted it, so I went for it."

"And at the clearing?"

"You'd almost died twice, Cherry. I wouldn't leave it to chance. I took enough to know this bond would last. That I wouldn't lose you again."

I should be livid. He'd made the decision for me *twice*. *To protect me*. As if I were a helpless little girl, and not a vampire who could stand on her own two feet—and kick ass, when need arose.

But his last words… His eyes, swirling with color that I knew corresponded to pain and hunger and even love…

He didn't want to lose me, and more than once he'd gone above and beyond, to keep me safe and happy.

I closed the distance between us and touched my lips to his cheek. *"I forgive you."* I tried to think it at him, unsure how this worked.

He slid his hands up my arms, his touch lighting my skin on fire. When he reached my shoulders, he dug in his fingers, holding me to him.

"I'll make you happy, if it kills me."

The emotion in his words slammed into my chest and made me lightheaded. It took all my willpower not to think of a response. I couldn't trust myself not to project it to him, and I didn't know what it would be, when my gut reaction was to lose myself in him.

He nuzzled my cheek. "I made so many mistakes as your mentor. I fancied myself a sort of Pygmalion and tried to sculpt the perfect woman out of you, when I should have spent our time together letting you know you already were perfect. *Are* perfect." And then—with the slightest tilt of his head—he found my lips and claimed them.

His soft, full lips glided against mine, before his talented tongue slid between them and caressed mine. My body melted against his, my heart still absorbing his words as I skated my palms up his sides, enjoying the hardness of his muscles beneath his smooth skin.

It was perfect.

I was kissing Constantine again, after so long. After I was sure he and I were done.

After I'd spent days thinking of another man.

I said I wouldn't wait for Alex, but part of me wanted us to fix things. To regain the normal, easy relationship we had before Willoughby and Ádísa threw us the mother of all curveballs.

With great reluctance and even greater regret, I broke the kiss. "Too soon," I said.

He ghosted his thumb over my cheek. "Will it ever not be?"

I had no reply for that. "Is it okay if I still stay here?" I asked after a second.

"Of course." His smile lit up the room.

"And you'll tell me about the whole vampire-to-human reversion thing?"

The smile wilted. When it reappeared, it didn't reach his eyes. "Anything to make you happy."

Cherry Vampire, Book 3 – Cherry Pie

What if you get what you want and it's not what you need?

I never asked to be a vampire, so when Constantine says there's a way for me and Alex to become human again, I jump at the chance. Alex's reservations may have something to do about the process's involving Constantine and me in bed together, but what's one night when I can have my life back?

And I plan to live that life with the man I love. I'll be mortal with Alex, and I couldn't be happier about it. Kinda. This would be much easier if mortality didn't come with pains and aches, and Alex wasn't pressuring me to start a family.

For too long others have made my choices for me. This is my chance to do what makes me happy. But first I have to decide what that is. And then I need to find the strength to claim it, before my options are taken away.

Acknowledgments

Thank you, Melina, for getting me a laptop when mine gave up on me. I wouldn't have written this without you. Thank you, Allyson Lindt and Sofia Grey for beta reading, cheerleading, and virtually kicking my ass when needed. Thank you, January M. for being the best content editor ever, and always making time for me and my stories. Thank you, Diane Saxon, for making this a much smoother read.

Thank you, Andrei for everything. I love you.

Last but not least, a great big thank you to everyone who read Cherry Stem and asked for more. I hope Alex didn't break your heart.

About the Author

Sotia loves romances with a twist and urban fantasy novels, always with vivid erotic elements. Her favorite characters to write are not conventional hero-material at first glance, and she enjoys making them fight for their happiness.

She shares her life and living quarters with her husband, their son, and two rescue dogs, one of which may be part-pony. Sappy movies make her bawl like a baby, and she wishes she could take in all the stray dogs in the world.

Also, she hates mornings.